I0549021

SYBIL NORCROFT MEETS THE DEVIL

Sybil's Private and Public Battle with
Beelzebub The Magnificent

Sybil Norcroft Book Seven

CARL DOUGLASS

Neurosurgeon turned Author who writes with
Gripping Realism

PUBLICATION
CONSULTANTS
We Believe In The Power Of Authors

PO Box 221974 Anchorage, Alaska 99522-1974
books@publicationconsultants.com, www.publicationconsultants.com

ISBN Number: 978-1-59433-938-7
eBook ISBN Number: 978-1-59433-939-4

Library of Congress Number: 2020933397

Copyright 2020 Carl Douglass
—First Edition—

All rights reserved, including the right of
reproduction in any form, or by any mechanical
or electronic means including photocopying or
recording, or by any information storage or
retrieval system, in whole or in part in any
form, and in any case not without the
written permission of the author and publisher.

Manufactured in the United States of America

BOOKS BY CARL DOUGLASS
Neurosurgeon Who Writes with Gripping Realism

FICTION

Last Phoenix-A Novel of Betrayal and Revenge, A Story of the CIA's Phoenix Program
Gog and Magog—Yawm al-Qiyamah, Yawm al-Din, The Day of Judgment
Sheep Dog and The Wolf-A Story of Terrorism and Response, and the Sheep Dogs Who Protect

Trojan Horse in the Belly of the Beast, **Three Books:**
  - *Though They Come From the Ends of the Earth-Book One*
  - *Dancing with the Devil-Book Two*
  - *Trojan Horse in the Belly of the Beast-Book Three*

Finders Keepers, Losers Weep-A Novel of Innocence Betrayed and the Search for Restitution
Gog and Magog—Yawm al-Qiyamah, Yawm al-Din, The Day of Judgment

Saga of a Neurosurgeon Series, **Six Books:**
  - *Young Coyote-Book One: Garven Wilsonhulme's Way to Success-No Quarter Asked and None Given*
  - *Anything Goes-Book Two*
  - *Heaven and Hell-Book Three: Garven Wilsonhulme Takes on All Comers in the Jungle of Modern Competition*

NOVELLAS (Twelve)

Sybil Series	McGee Series
1st Novella-*The End of the Beginning*	1st Novella-*Friends at Homeland Security*
2ndNovella- *Uncharted Country, Uncertain Future*	2nd Novella-*Crossing the Cult*
3rd Novella-*Secrets*	3rd Novella-*Wednesday's Child*
4th Novella-*Secrets and Scandals*	4th Novella-*Death on a Pale Horse*
5thNovella-*Decisions*	5th Novella-*The Boss's Daughters*
6thNovella-*Running with the Big Dogs* 7thNovella-*Sybil Norcroft Meets the Devil*	6th Novella—*Another Whistle Blower*

NONFICTION

On Evolution and *Something about Religion*
Both out of print

DISCLAIMER

This book is fiction; the characters are the products of the author's imagination and are not persons who ever lived. Any resemblance to the characters and actual people, or of the story to actual events would be purely coincidental and unintentional.

DEDICATION

To Evan Swensen's Author Masterminds–
the best of the best in their respective genres.

CHAPTER ONE

Sybil Norcroft had listened to the President of the United States deliver a verbal bombshell. She was always ambitious, but that request by President Willets was a shock to the woman of ice who was currently serving as the director of the Central Intelligence Agency. His precise statement had been: "Sybil, I am all but certain that Randall Broome will be the next president of the United States and Dick Harris his vice-president. I have two secrets I want to share with you since you are my most trusted mistress of the vault of secrets and chief of the puzzle palace."

She had smiled at his characterization of herself and her agency.

He had continued, "What I have to tell you must never be repeated...Harris is very ill, and no one else but Governor Broome and I know that. He just found out two weeks ago, and it is too late to get a new V-P at this late date. The best estimate by his doctors is that the poor man will have to resign for health reasons before the end of his first year in office."

Sybil digested every word, waiting almost without breathing for the next sentence—the virtual next shoe to drop.

President Willets did not disappoint her, "And Governor Broome has mild to moderate congestive heart failure—that's another top secret—his prognosis is not all that good so far as I have been told. I owe him my place in the White House and could never do or say anything that would deny him his chance. He has been a real patriot and has the good of the nation foremost in everything he does."

The president looked directly into Sybil's intent eyes, "He and I have discussed the need for him to appoint you to the vice-presidency when the time comes for Harris to step down."

He paused to allow Sybil to digest the import of what he was telling her.

She said, "Mr. President, I would be proud to serve. You know I would do anything for you."

She was well known to be a woman who chose her words very carefully and to be a person whose word was her bond, as old-fashioned as that might sound in these unsettled times.

"Thank you, Sybil. I know you would. I am sure that you know—should my expectations come to pass—you will become the first woman ever to serve in that high office, just like you were the first woman to serve as the DCIA. I think it highly unlikely that you will ever be the first lady, but with the conditions of politics and the health of the two aspirants in head of you, it is not outside the realms of probability that you will become the first woman to occupy the west wing as its leader and likely will be the first woman of the nation not so long afterward. I am pretty certain that your political career is not over, my friend."

Sybil remembered that she must have looked like the proverbial deer looking at approaching headlights, "Who knows about such things, Mr. President, who knows?" was all she could manage.

For the next few afternoons, Sybil used a rare period of relative quiet in the spy world to ponder the implication of the president's information and his offer. She had always been convinced that the vice-presidency was "not worth a bucket of warm spit." [actually, the word V-P John Nance Garner had used was not considered appropriate for polite society] However, she did feel a strong affinity to the current president and was willing to serve him even in an enervating position if that was what he needed. The dangle of becoming the potential president after next was tantalizing to her. That she could not deny.

The chief of police of Los Angeles received a letter that was destined to change Sybil Norcroft's life in ways she could not have imagined as she contemplated the possibility of taking on one of the highest of responsibilities. The letter was originally sent to the editor of the Los Angeles Times, but the editor was loathe to print it because of its inflammatory nature. He referred it to Chief Anderson,

11

who elected to keep it secret to allow his detective bureau to find the potential killer or absurd crank without causing a panic in California.

That decision blew up in Chief Anderson's face when the threats contained in the letter came true, and he and his chief of D's had not a clue who the letter writer and probable killer was. Two synagogues and a Beth Israel Temple kindergarten class were bombed with dozens of innocent victims, and an African-American reverend had been shot to death in his church. Chief Anderson was no fool, and he did not have any intention of taking the blame for any failures to identify and to bring the monster to justice. He made a bold move: he requested that the directors of the FBI and the CIA assume authority for the investigation with help from Los Angeles and the State of California.

Chief Anderson attached a copy of the hand-written letter that started all the angst to the two directors with an expression of his firm conviction that they were dealing with a probable monster and mass murderer.

"You don't need to know my name. I go by Beelzebub, and I am the Magnificent. You will know all you need to know soon. Soon enough. You think Teddy B. who thought he was so smart, will be remembered. Forget that. Wait until I make the news. Anybody remember Timothy McVeigh, the Oklahoma Fed building bombing as dramatic as it was? Or Wade Michael Page, who blew up a bunch of rag-head Sikhs in one of what they dare to call their "temples", or Dylann Roof, who killed a bunch of what we're now supposed to call African-Americans in Charleston Church, or Robert Bowers, who took down Pittsburgh synagogue in Pittsburgh? None of those heroes that carried out the work of God are still in the news, still remembered, still revered— except by me, I suppose.

"If you go back a bit, there are a whole bunch of our kind of people—WASPS, nationalists, real populists, true blood segregationists who hardly get a mention in the news media of today, despite the great work they did. Those workers just didn't go about the publicity angle good enough. Maybe they weren't educated enough, or smart enough, or had the stick-to-itiveness that was needed. Well, things are gonna change. I am smarter, better educated— don't bother looking it up, I'm what you'd call self-educated—better organized, and more driven to get the job done for the good white folks of the country and for the rest of the world.

"When Beelzebub, the Magnificent, makes his mark; and he will–believe you me– he (really, that's me), will never be forgotten and will hold a great place in American and world history. Then–in the shrine that will get built–you'll all get to hold dear the names of heroes and martyrs like: The noble Klansmen and segregationists—Thomas Edwin Blanton Jr., Herman Frank Cash, Robert Edward Chambliss, and Bobby Frank Cherry, who showed their courage and conviction at the African American 16th Street Baptist Church in Birmingham, Alabama, and the Mississippi Burning heroic action that got rid of three leftie Eastern activists back in June, 1964. You gotta laugh when you learn that it was actual Neshoba County Mississippi cops who did us that favor. It was during the so-called Civil Rights Era. They disposed of the traitor to his kind, James Chaney, from up around Meridian, Mississippi, Andrew Goodman—sounds like a Jew–and Michael "Mickey" Schwerner—a radical Jew, of course–from New York City—of course. Let the names of those invaders of the true South be forgotten, the White Knights of the Ku Klux Klan be emblazoned in your hearts, brothers.

"They are: Cecil Price, Samuel Bowers, Alton Wayne Roberts, Jimmy Snowden, Billy Wayne Posey, Horace Barnette, Jimmy Aldredge, and Edgar Ray Killen. They all went through Kangaroo trials held in secret by Jew lawyers and African-American judges—every one of them. You won't read that in the news, and all the records about them have mysteriously "disappeared".

"Our people have been at the work for a long time. I'll give you some history; you can forget trying to Google this; the dark side left has already expunged the records. Try to remember these heroes: the Armed Resistance Unit who carried off the audacious bombings of the U.S. Senate Building, three military installations around D.C., and four enemy sites in New York City. Their names were Marilyn Jean Buck, Linda Sue Evans, Susan Rosenberg, Timothy Blunk, Alan Berkman, and Elizabeth Ann Duke—all good real American names. I checked all of them out. I have my sources, trust me. And there was Paul Hasson from Maryland. He was a true White Nationalist Coast Guard lieutenant who got fed up with all the commies, Jews, Papists, and atheists, who run the country. In February, 2019, he carefully planned of plotting targeted assassinations of high-ranked liberal—or do we have to call them progressives now?—Holly Weird, and fake news alt-left, antifa, ideology of death, celebs. Brother Paul had some well-chosen, medium and high value targets. He had the arms and even biological weapons he got from brothers in the CIA secret biological labs. Some commie ratted him out on trumped up (no pun-intended, haha) weapons and drug possession before he could get his great work done. So, of course, his contribution to American history has been tucked away in some so-called "classified" archive in Langley.

I would wish that you could have a little shrine place in the sanctity of your White Christian homes to honor Gordon Kahl, a Posse Comitatus brother, who killed two federal marshals who were illegally hounding him. Then, they murdered him. Include in your sacred shrine Eric Rudolph who executed a series of daring attacks back in the late nineties (ancient history, right?). He did the 1996 Centennial Olympic Park bombing—which killed two, and injured 111. You could ask why? Why the Games? I'll tell you. It was to cancel the games, because they promote global socialism and communism. He knew he would embarrass the U.S. government and get us out of the foreign involvement business. The man was a prolific hero. He bombed an abortion clinic in Sandy Springs, Atlanta, the Otherside Lounge—dirty name–an Atlanta lesbian bar, in 1997, and an abortion clinic in Birmingham. The man was a hero, but I bet you can't remember him. When I am finished, people will flock to the All

American, All White, All Christian schools and libraries to learn about Brother Eric and the rest.

I'm coming; and when I come, the landscape will change. It will be America for Americans—real White heterosexual Americans, and an America where our White Children are safe from integration, stupid leftist ideas, and the enemies of the real America. Did I say it would be easy? Oh, no sir. I did not. I will start the way, show the way, and lead the way. My name will be written in the hymnals of the real Christian religion, and there won't be any other foreign religions left in the country.

Be afraid. I'm coming. Know that I am the Lord of the Earth, Beelzebub, and I am Magnificent. You won't know when or where; but you will remember when I do. And you will love the new America I bring—unless you happen not belong to the White, Christian, Protestant, conservative, flag-loving (Confederate and U.S. only), and have the right thoughts, hahaha.

Signed:

Beelzebub, The Magnificent

Hahaha

CHAPTER TWO

S ybil gritted her teeth as she read the odious message from the potential mass murderer. If she did not have a position of significant law enforcement responsibility, she might have shunted the problem of dealing with the weirdo to the LAPD or left it to the FBI. But she could not forget her experience with the diabolical pharmaceutical company operating from the Congo, which threatened untold millions of people around the world. She had worked with FBI, police forces, military units, French, Canadian, English, and American, law enforcement; and together, they had brought the massive criminal enterprise down. She had been personally and directly involved, even having to kill. Sybil had vowed never again to allow herself to get directly involved; after all, she was the boss, and she had personnel who worked for her who could handle it well. That would be the easy way.

She knew she was losing her argument with herself and thought that was absurd; but she also knew that in the currently politically charged and extreme political correctness society, she would have to start low and to go slow. She started with a letter to Chief Anderson, LAPD, with whom she had worked before and sent a copy to Landon Murphy, the DFBI.

Chief Lawrence Anderson, Los Angeles Police Department

Larry: I studied your letter regarding the Beelzebub character multiple times and came to the conclusion, as I am sure you did, that this is a credible threat to at least the national security of the United States. I have dealt with many such threats during my career. Too often, they are written off as lunatics, or zealots for some cause or another that have become unhinged. I have determined that that is rare. Whatever drives this Beelzebub, it is not likely to be mental illness, or even ideology, despite his alt-right rantings. Whatever resources we have, you are welcome to; but you know that I cannot get the Company involved in strictly domestic affairs, especially when it appears that we are dealing with an American, and a citizen at that. Get Landon Murphy and his feds involved now; don't try to handle it alone. The minute this monster indicates a multi- or transnational involvement, my department and I will join with all our might.

I would wish you good luck, if I believed in that sort of thing. I do believe in you and your superb officers. Please keep me in the loop.

Signed: Your colleague, Sybil Norcroft

As soon as she completed the letter and wired it off through secure lines, Sybil wanted to kick herself for her timidity. However, she had worked in Washington long enough to know that it was more than her career was worth to get involved in what was likely to turn out as a sensational media circus without having an international element to give her an entre. It was not as if she was swamped with demanding crises around the world. Her PDBs [Presidential Daily Briefings] with President Willets had become comparatively dull for the last month or so. The two of them had a little laugh over that, done with crossed fingers.

The next outrage was predictable. It took place in Milwaukee during a peaceful march by a group of striking public high school teachers. A haphazard collection of skin-heads and neo-nazis marched along Main Street headed directly towards the strikers. Both groups had city parade permits. The confrontational attitude of the alt-right marchers was evident by the Confederate, Aryan Supremacy, and Nazi, flags they waved and their racist and anti-Semitic signage. The two determined groups came face-to-face in front of a large Walmart store.

The two groups hardly had time to call out their rhetoric when two bombs exploded—one on each end of the marchers–causing panic, confusion, injures, and nearly 100 deaths on each end. Teachers and skin-heads alike were victims. The talking heads on the news did not know what to make of that fact; so, they chose their usual sides and vilified the left or the right as was their wont to do. The local police called in the FBI, and together they pledged to bring the perpetrator or perpetrators to justice in a coordinated effort. The only saving grace was that the incident did not appear to have significant racial overtones.

The Milwaukee "incident" was characterized as the work of political extremists, terrorists, disgruntled employees, and lunatics—all without evidence. After the usual five-day news cycle, interest faded, as it usually does.

Interest rekindled when The *Milwaukee Journal Sentinel* daily morning broadsheet published a letter from an unknown character who called himself "Beelzebub" on day six. Because interest had been so intense initially, the editors elected to publish it on the front page above the fold.

> "I heard nothing from my first letter to the *LA Times*; so, maybe this'll get your attention. I warned you that Beelzebub was on his way. Well, I'm here. I done it; the lefties and the right-wingers both got a dose. Speculate, make stupid ideas, or call in every cop from this country and from the rest of the world; but there's nothing you can do. THE END IS NEAR!"
> Beelzebub, The Magnificent
> Ha, ha, ha

With that newspaper announcement, the editor of the *LA Times* informed the LA chief of police that they would print the original letter. Chief Anderson agreed and allowed a short statement from him to be placed in a side-bar, "The

LA Police Department is aware of this dangerous individual or group and is actively involved in an investigation with the support and cooperation of the FBI."

Those two newspapers with their millions of subscribers lit a fire of interest in Beelzebub. Preachers, ideologues, talk shows, commentators, and news outlets, saturated the nation's airwaves. Sybil and her co-horts in law enforcement cringed and prepared for worse.

It did not take long. Bombs and letters from Beelzebub popped up in a deadly deluge over the next month. Bombings made the news in the *Salt Lake Tribune* [re: The recently renovated public library which was holding a celebration—sixty two wounded, twenty-two killed], *The Minneapolis Star Tribune* [re: a hip-hop concert by the Rampagers in the Armory Music Venue—112 wounded, sixty-four killed], *Albany, New York Times Union* [re: the Vintage Bad Boys opening in the Hollow—fifty-six wounded, eighteen killed], and in the *Odessa American* newspaper in Odessa, Texas [re: three explosions in the Ratliff Stadium during the yearly Odessa-Midland grudge high school football game—284 wounded, 177 killed].

Aside from the different venues in the different cities, the MO was disturbingly familiar. The fuses and detonators evaluated by the FBI were nearly clones of each other; letters sent to the various newspapers were undeniably from the same person—same writing style, paper from the same batch of German-made expensive writing paper, identical signatures as confirmed by FBI handwriting experts, and with the first new letter, a well-executed

21

symbol of a horned devil surrounded by official symbols of six different religions from around the developed world. Beelzebub demanded that his symbol be kept secret ["it is copyrighted" he said]; so, his letters and his great work could be verified.

CHAPTER THREE

It was no great surprise when another of those "make-you-nervous" calls came via the blinking red lights of the secure line. She had been expecting this particular call.

Sybil took a deep breath and picked it up on the second ring.

"This is a secure line."

"Is this you, Sybil?" came the very familiar voice of POTUS, Parker Conrad Willets.

"Yes, Mr. President."

"Can you give me anything...anything...on this Beelzebub terrorist, Sybil? This is becoming a political nightmare as well as colossal human tragedy."

"Not yet, Sir. We have made him or her our first priority and so has the FBI. Nada. Regular channels including Interpol, the intelligence, diplomatic, and security services of every civilized country have come up dry. We're still at it, but whoever this is has no digital signature or address, no criminal record, and none of our assets in the white supremacist circles has ever heard of such a character."

"Is this terrorism?"

"Apparently, not exactly, that is, not by the technical definition. He or she doesn't have a consistent axe to grind or message to trumpet. Beelzebub doesn't credit any known group for the outrages. His modus operandi is basically chaotic; nobody can get a handle on how he does things. Worse, we cannot predict anything about the next set of victims."

"Have you had a chat with the Russians and the Chinese—the usual suspects?"

"No, and not for lack of trying. It won't come as any surprise to you, but the Russians are enjoying a Cold War with us, and the Chinese have been thrilled beyond measure that the last administration cut us off from any meaningful interchange with them. The South China Sea and Southeast Asia is their sphere of interest, and they are flexing their muscles everywhere and every time they get a chance. That includes not bothering to return calls or messages. We are working at getting to them through back doors, but no luck yet."

"Well, Sybil, I sure am glad I called and got cheered up," President Willets said, "I think I'll go up to the residence, assume the fetal position, and turn the electric blanket up to nine."

"That sounds like a luxury, Mr. President. Given the level of concern and threat, may I assume that I have near carte blanche to do spy wizardry to get places I shouldn't, Sir?"

"Do what you have to do, Sybil. I trust you."

That afternoon, a new development, a terrible one, but with some promise of a new avenue to explore took place. The New York Stock Exchange main frame was hacked. In fact, it was held up for ransom—one billion dollars, payable in one week, or the cost would be two billion. If the ransom was not paid at that time, the "kidnappers" promised to crash the entire system and to divert the holdings of the Exchange.

To prove to the New York executives that the kidnappers were both serious and capable, the town of Rincon, South Carolina went through the same set of ransom threat, repeat threat, and as of yesterday, every financial asset of the town and Jesse Jackson County disappeared without a trace. The FBI finally followed what appeared to be an intentional digital trail to the Ministry of State Security [MSS]—the intelligence, security and secret police agency of the PRC [People's Republic of China] for nonmilitary interests.

It was obviously no coincidence that a letter signed by Beelzebub, The Magnificent, appeared the same afternoon–written in Mandarin Chinese. After translation into English, it was printed in the *People's Daily* and the *China Daily*. It was printed untranslated in its original form in *Beijing Morning Post* with a web site in the Chinese language, the *Beijing Evening News*, the *Beijing News*, and the *Global Times* with a daily circulation of 1,042,000, making it one of the biggest newspapers in the world.

PEOPLE'S DAILY, November 12,
Dear citizens of Beijing, did you think you could escape my great eye? How silly of you. And bad joss. I will visit your evil country soon, and you will regret all your communist sins. I am the great end-times avenger. Live in fear and trembling.
– Beelzebub, The Magnificent
Hahaha

The PRC public was very well informed about Beelzebub from reprints of the letters from western outlets and from news articles and commentaries approved by the party. The general gist of the news the Chinese had been absorbing was that an irate and downtrodden victim of the imperialist bandits had broken his fetters and was lashing back at the capitalist hegemonists. The new take was that Beelzebub was threatening the PRC because Russia and America had bought him off. The editorialists scoffed at the thought that a lunatic could succeed in his terrorism while the great Chinese nation was protected by the MSS and PLA [People's Liberation Army].

On November 13, at noon, near a disputed island named Sandy Cay [Philippine-occupied island called Pagasa by Filipinos], two destroyers from a flotilla of 200 Chinese naval vessels were sunk by explosions from limpet mines. The Chinese accused the Filipinos; Philippine President Dutarte assailed the Chinese for "perpetrating a hoax to inflame world opinion". The United States ordered the Seventh Fleet to the area, and Russia began fly-overs with its a large, four-engine turboprop-powered strategic bomber and missile platform Tupolev_Tu-95. All sabers were rattling.

Fanning the growing fire, a missive from a largely unknown person in the Philippine Islands was printed in the *Manilla Bulletin* and the *Manilla Times*, written in Tagalog per the demands of the secret submitter, a letter which shifted blame and interest.

> *Manilla Bulletin*, November 13
> Dear citizens of the Philippine Islands, did you think you could escape the wrath of the Chinese? Do you now think you can evade my great eye? How silly of you all. And *malas* [tagalog: bad luck]? I will visit your own evil country soon, and you will regret all your sins of being the lapdogs of the Great Satan, America. I am the great end-times avenger. The fool Chinese are but my tools. Live in fear and trembling. Look overhead for my people. Look to the sea for your enemy.
> - Beelzebub, The Magnificent
> Hahaha

The latest atrocities resulted in 3,123 Chinese sailors and marines KIA and presumed lost at sea. The financial loss was a closely held national secret by the PRC. The plight of the financially ruined little South Carolina city of Rincon was largely eclipsed by the international crisis, but the town essentially died when all its money and services evaporated in a single key-stroke.

The shock-waves were not over: the NYSE announced that hackers, presumably from Red China, had caused a billion dollars to disappear into the dark digital cloud without so much as a set of 0-1, 1-0 hints as to where.

DCIA Norcroft was alarmed and sprang into action. She made two encrypted telephone calls, the first to Dr. Steven Highnam, the director of DARPA [Defense Advanced Research Projects Agency].

"Hello, Dr. Norcroft, to what do I owe the pleasure of this call, my co-conspirator?" the director said as soon as the two secure lines were connected.

"No pleasure, Steven, I'm afraid; and I don't suppose you were expecting any. I am sure you know all about this Beelzebub entity—probably more than me. The Firm is getting nowhere. We need all the help we can get. First off, can you get a look at the encrypted messages he or she sent? Find us a signature, or an IP address, or something that identifies the monster or even where the messages come from."

"We're already on it. What we found is not of any help it seems. The signature is hidden all over in the encryptions—Beelzebub, The Magnificent. No surprises or real intel there. The digital track is circular—pings from stations all around the globe and back again. This is likely a state sponsor. It seems like too much work for an individual, however smart or handy with the keyboard he or she is."

"Pretty thin, Steven. Any idea what state sponsor?"

"Certainly not yet. Could be Russian government, the *vory v zakone* [*russaya mafiya*], or the very quickly advancing Chinese, even the Philippine president's office.

He hates us enough. I wouldn't rule out organized crime from anywhere in the world, or the Islamic militants. I am going to assign my deputy, Peter Walker, to head up things at our end. He'll be working with the spooks at the Tactical Technology Office; that gives us both a defensive and an offensive channel. I presume you can get the necessary approvals from the president, Madam Director?

"I'll take care of it, Steven."

Sybil's next call was to a long dormant agent with whom she had worked previously. He knew were all the bodies were buried or hidden, and everything about everyone who mattered in black ops world.

CHAPTER FOUR

It took Sybil four cutouts to reach the subject of her next conversation, and that took almost a full twenty-four hours.

"Garcia's *Uyuni* Bar and Grill," was the answer when Sybil was finally able to make telephone contact.

Her secure room monitor identified the location as the Salt Block Hotel in the town of Uyuni in the *Salar de Uyuni* [Salted Earth] Bolivia. The place was an extremely important but flat, desolate, and dangerous, corner of the highly contested lithium triangle of South America, and the world's largest salt flat. The Lithium Triangle is located at the corner where Chile, Bolivia, and Argentina, meet. Chile owns the largest part of the lithium rich area, with its boundaries where the *Salar de Atacamba* and the *Salar de Uyuni* link up with the northern ends of Argentina and Bolivia. *Salar de Uyuni* is in the Daniel Campos Province in Potosí in southwest Bolivia, near the crest of the Andes.

"May I speak to Mr. Howard?"

"I will see if the *jefe* is here."

"Please do, it is important."

"*Yo entiendo—muy importante.*"

Ten minutes later a gruff male voice picked up, "Code," it said without further civilities.

Sybil gave her most secret coded PIN, known only to POTUS and the DNI [Director, National Intelligence].

"What's so important that the ODNI gave you my location, Sybil? On second thought, this is not a secure line. I'm afraid you'll need to come and see me under cover as a tourist; so, we can talk. Is it worth that?"

"Yes."

"Then, I'll make myself available. Nice to talk to you, Boss. ETA?"

"Tomorrow early. I will fly into Sucre or La Paz on the Firm's jet, then hire a private plane to get to Uyuni."

"Copy that."

The receiver at his end clicked off the conversation. Lincoln Howard–as Sybil knew him–was on assignment for the ODNI, and reported only to the director himself. He had a Coded Q Clearance, the highest clearance shared only with the very most senior intelligence officers. His clearance allowed access to Classified information up to and including TOP SECRET data with the special designation: Restricted Data (TS//RD)

Before making the call, Sybil had gotten clearance from POTUS and the Office of the Director National Intelligence. If she could persuade him with her high office and not insignificant charms, he would be on loan for the duration.

One of the great perks of her office is that she had access to the same customized Boeing 757-200 and Boeing 737 aircraft which carry the military designation C-32A and C-40B as POTUS, VPOTUS, the Secretaries of State and Defense and the DNI.

It only took a call to the White House Military Office for arrangements, and Sybil was able to board a better plane than the one the Firm could supply. She boarded the plane at Andrews Air Force Base the following day and traveled in air-conditioned comfort to high altitude La Paz without anyone else—even her top aides—knowing where she was.

The jet landed in the diplomatic section El Alto International Airport in La Paz, *Estado Plurinacional de Bolivia.* The capital is Sucre; but the financial, executive, and legislative center, is La Paz. Company agents quickly saw to it that the official American airplane was secretly and securely ensconced in a hangar well out of the high traffic areas of the airport.

The ODNI had prearranged a flight on an old—no longer in regular service—Fairchild Swearingen Metroliner—a sixteen passenger pressurized, twin-turboprop, airliner, produced in a plant in San Antonio, Texas and currently owned by an Air America subsidiary. The flight from La Paz to *Salar de Uyuni* on the small *Línea Aérea Amaszonas* plane was a bit bumpy and altogether devoid of amenities, but it served Sybil's strict time schedule very well. There was a total of twelve other tourists on the flight.

Three attractive young women met the passengers as they deplaned and walked into the tiny waiting room/waiting center of the airport, which barely lived up to the appellation. They each carried a placard advertising their three separate touring companies. Those tour groups accounted for everyone but Sybil, who took a trip to the ladies' room to avoid standing out alone and stayed there for as long as she could hold her breath.

A tall, wiry, sun-bronzed, man with prematurely white hair stood by the cigarette vending machine. His face had the topographical permanent lines of a man who had spent long days in the bright sun. It was not the look of a country-club tennis player, rather it was the hard face of a man who had only serious intentions and did not sanction nonsense. He wore light colored cotton Bermuda shorts, a loose-fitting SPF shirt, white cotton socks, and scuffed rubber soled hiking shoes. She recognized him immediately but did not acknowledge his presence; nor did he give her so much as a nod.

He turned and walked out the back entrance of the building. She waited until he was going through the door before moving to follow him. He moved swiftly to a beat-up old jeep and got into the driver's seat. Sybil checked all around then moved directly to the jeep and got into the shotgun seat.

"Think this wreck will get us wherever you have in mind to go, Lincoln?" Sybil asked with winning smile.

"And hello to you, too, Sybil. How's your day been?"

She laughed.

"It is good to see you. How much do you know about why I'm here?"

"Not a whole lot. I was left to assume that it was some top-secret caper or other that you've dreamed up."

"Close. Drive, and I'll tell you everything I know."

She filled him in about everything she knew about Beelzebub, the Magnificent: his zany letters to newspapers, his mass murders, and his odd changes of things and people to rant about and to attack.

"So this guy…person or entity, is a good old boy Confederate states born again who hates all people who don't share his religion and political ideology. He hates Jews, blacks, browns, Americans, Catholics, police, military, diplomats, Chinese, Filipinos, the CIA, teachers, and skin-heads. Did I miss anything or anyone?"

"Both capitalists and communists."

Lincoln shook his head. He stopped so they could take in the view. It had rained the previous day, and two or three inches of rain sat on the gleaming salt flats, making it into a gigantic mirror. Further ahead, near the center of the great salt flat was a set of several conical hills poking their heads out of the salt flats–the remains of ancient volcanoes submerged during the era of Lake Minchin. When they reached the Lake–enlarged and made deeper by the rain—Sybil was awed by the incredible mirror spreading out in front of the low volcanic top. The water was absolutely still and flat as glass. The mirror image of the hill in the water was perfect. Sybil took five photos on her iPhone and hoped no one would be able to make anything out of the fact that those pictures were there or would even know where "there" was.

"I presume you've told me everything you know, Sybil. Not much to go on. I take it that you've come a long way to get me involved. What do you want from me?"

"I know how you work, and how well you work. I remember how you once told me about a quote from Seneca. He was quoting Hannibal. The Carthaginian general and his army were plodding their painful way up the Italian Alps to launch a surprise attack on unsuspecting Romans. It was approaching winter; it was cold and slippery. Mules, elephants, and men were falling off the narrow trail to their deaths. The entire effort seemed futile to the generals. One evening, they took Hannibal aside and shared their doubts.

"How are you going to overcome the terrible obstacles the gods have put in front of you, General?" they asked.

"He gave a profound answer which Seneca recorded in Latin: '*Aut enveniam viam aut faciam.*' In English, that was, 'I will find a way or make one.'

"I liked your work ethic then, and I need it now. I want you to drop everything and come back to civilization and help me to find this devil and to deal with him or whatever it is. We can figure out exactly what to do while we are flying to D.C. What do you say?"

"Did POTUS and DNI order it?"

"Not exactly, but I have full discretion; and I can make it an order, if I have to. I'd rather we worked as partners to get this monster away from humans and to cancel the slide into a war as stupid as World War I and even more terrible."

"You know that what I'm doing is also crucial. Lithium is a key ingredient in lightweight batteries and is already powering the modern world. It is probably the key to getting the world to reduce its reliance on fossil fuels. Under its dense, several centimeters deep salt crust, the Salar de Uyuni is also the world's biggest single deposit of lithium, accounting for maybe half of the world's resources of the precious alkaline metal. Lithium is an ideal material for light-weight batteries; it is the most energy dense of battery materials. It stores the most energy for a given weight. It is also crucial for the treatment of manic-depressive disorder. I have a son with it. It is terrible.

"Right now, there is no mining plant currently at the best sites, and the Bolivian government won't allow exploitation by foreign corporations or governments. It has plenty of suitors. Instead, it intends to build its own pilot plant with a modest annual production of 1,200 tons of lithium, and to increase it to 30,000 tons in four years. They hate us and want to cut us out entirely, make us beg and kneel. We can't let that happen, even if we have to start a war. I am making progress, maybe even to get a coup going that will come out favoring us. I can't go now, not now!" Lincoln stressed.

"I don't deny that what you are doing is crucially important, Lincoln, but it is not an emergency; and this is. The DNI can get along without you, He can replace you temporarily."

"Maybe it sounds stupid or arrogant, but I am crucial here. I won't leave. You would have to order me officially."

Sybil was not known as the "Ice Queen" or the "Snow Queen" for nothing.

Her countenance became calm, firm, and cold. She spoke quietly, calmly, and in a small voice that penetrated into Lincoln's core.

"You are so ordered. Get in the car; we are leaving."

CHAPTER FIVE

It was a very quiet ride for the two spies; scarcely a word passed between them during the flight from *Salar de Uyuni* to La Paz to Miami, and from there to Beijing, where the most recent egregious attacks had occurred by the Beelzebub terrorist. Lincoln's roiling temper cooled down enough by the time they landed at PEK [Beijing International Airport] on West Jichang Road for him to take the high road and ask Sybil their purpose for coming to the PRC.

Sybil gifted her agent with her prize-winning smile as if she always traveled in silence and with a frown.

She said, "Well, Lincoln, I trust you slept well. It will be a busy time for us, I think."

He raised a questioning eyebrow.

"Oh, yes, why China? First–at the moment–they would appear to have the most to gain by this strange pattern of murderous attacks. Second, they have one of the top five best intelligence agencies—better at attacks than we are, Lincoln. Third, it is my personal opinion that their hacking capabilities are better than anyone in the western world, and maybe even better than the so highly touted Russian teenagers."

"I don't dispute any of that, but what do you think they are trying to accomplish?"

"I am never quite sure what the Chinese are thinking. Better men than me have tried and failed to get a good handle on their thought processes and why they do what they do. Remember, Lincoln, they have been around for thousands of years doing much the same thing. I think the U S of A can ill afford what they are doing."

"Sure, so what will it cost us to get to know what the commies are really up to?"

"Not so very much, Lincoln: a plane ride to Shanghai, a bit of a spy-like walk in a crowded city, and perhaps some money will change hands. I am confident that you and the guy I know will work together swimmingly. The two of you are going to supply me with a detailed description of just how the Chinese are involved, with whom, and why."

"Are we back to Sybil and Lincoln, Ma'am?"

"Never ma'am, Lincoln. I associate the title with untidy houses and bad women. So, let's be Sybil and Lincoln while we're getting along, all right?"

"Groovy," Lincoln responded and shined one of his most inviting smiles on his boss.

She laughed.

There were too many people everywhere for the two spooks to have a real conversation about the work they needed to get done. They flew from Beijing Nanyuan

Airport on China Eastern Airline. It was too late to go where Sybil wanted to go that night by the time they landed in SHA / ZSSS [Shanghai Hongqiao International Airport] which handled most of the domestic flights. By mutual agreement and because of good trade craft, they went separate ways for the night. It was not because of some antiquarian concept of avoiding hanky-panky; there was not a one of the 30,000 plus CIA agents in the world who would attempt anything remotely like a pass or would "make a move" on the attractive, but untouchable DCIA. She was the "Ice Queen" after all. To maintain her anonymity, Sybil took a cab to the Air China Shanghai Hongqiao Airport Hotel in terminal 2, less than half a mile away. Lincoln walked half a mile from terminal 1 to the Mercure Shanghai Hongqiao Airport. He needed to stretch his cramped legs, and he was among the world's lightest travelers.

The next morning early, they met in the quick travelers' café in the Air China hotel and ate a hearty fry up English breakfast in anticipation of a strenuous day of spying. Even dainty Sybil consumed the proteinaceous calories at pace with Lincoln who out-weighed her by sixty pounds: fried eggs, sausages, a rafter of back bacon, tomatoes, garlic and butter mushrooms, fried bread with marmalade, black pudding [~ bloodwurst], tea and coffee with cream and sugar, and hot, buttered toast.

Both Sybil and Lincoln casually looked around the crowded café. It was packed with Chinese families, and the noise was nearly deafening. The Chinese love to eat;

they love their families; and they love to be heard. To carry on any kind of conversation—let alone a whispered sharing between cautious spies—would have been impossible.

Instead, Sybil scribbled on two pieces of paper, and gave each to Lincoln in a covert gesture. On one, it read, "Lincoln=Hans Thomas; the other read, "Sybil=Mrs. North". Lincoln nodded his understanding, both of the pseudonyms they would be assuming during the day, and of the need to avoid "r's" and "l's" which were so difficult for Chinese to pronounce.

Lincoln casually flicked his cigarette lighter on and burned the papers to ashes in the ash tray on the table, then—for good measure—poured the remains of his coffee on the charred remnants.

Sybil gave him a directional signal with her lips—a useful gesture they picked up in South America—and walked away from the table and back to her room in the hotel. Lincoln followed at a discrete distance. Both made a few maze-like spy-craft moves to confuse would-be shadowers.

Sybil entered her room; and shortly, Lincoln walked past and turned into the service area as if he were seeking a bucket of ice. He checked twice; and, seeing no one in the hall, he doubled back and softly knocked on Sybil's room door in the prearranged Beethoven's Fifth Symphony leitmotif: "da da da dum, da da da dum, da da da," repeated three times.

Sybil opened the door suddenly and pointed a Glock .30 at Lincoln's chest. She put it away and pulled him in. He followed her to a dressing table facing a large, brightly lit mirror. An assortment of cosmetics, paints, powders, cosmetic pens, pencils, and wigs were arrayed on the table.

"Help me flatten my hair back as tight as we can get it," she asked.

That was no mean feat. Her hair was long, lustrous, heavy, and blond, matching her sharp Nordic features. Lincoln wet the hair thoroughly, applied heavy gel, and squeezed it into a cranial form-fitting cap. Then he put on a sooty-grey colored doo-rag to hold it in place. She applied aging theatrical paints and cosmetics which made her look like a woman of sixty. Unfortunately, she still looked like Sybil was going to look at that age.

"Big, old nose," Lincoln offered.

"Got one," Sybil said.

With care, Sybil became a fat cheeked, sallow-eyed, big nosed, old crone, with an indeterminate age of around seventy-five. Lincoln penciled in age lines and wrinkles which advanced her age another five years and added a decided touch of authenticity to the make-up result.

"Good enough?" Sybil asked.

"I would never be able to pick you out of a crowd," he replied after a studied look.

"Now, for some unsuitable, unfashionable, old, clothes."

Her laundry basket held four choices, and together, they found the perfectly believable frumpy frock.

The last step was to select, then to position, an elderly Chinese woman's wig. By then, no one who knew her would be able to recognize her if she sat next to them on a bus. She added an old pair of round lens glasses favored by elderly and proper Chinese ladies.

"Nice work, Sybil," said Lincoln. "You know the old saw about girls who wear glasses seldom rate passes. I think you are going to be perfectly safe."

"So, let us go out and enter the world of spies, liars, and villains," Sybil said as she hobbled towards the door.

CHAPTER SIX

Lincoln was dressed in a European-cut charcoal grey business suit, white shirt, conservative tie, communist sun red dress pocket square prominently displayed, and black wing-tipped Florsheim shoes—every bit the British businessman going about his appointed rounds that morning. Sybil sat inside a dingy little tea house two blocks away from the building of interest to them both— an imposing twelve-story building off Datong Road–in a public, mixed-use area of Pudong in Shanghai.

The building—known to every intelligence organization in the developed world—housed PLA Unit 61398– also variously known as APT 1, Comment Crew, Comment Panda, GIF89a, and Byzantine Candor–the MUCD [Military Unit Cover Designator] of the People's Liberation Army advanced persistent threat unit known by all to be the main source of Chinese computer hacking attacks. 61398 specialized in the theft of confidential business information and intellectual property from United States commercial firms and of planting malware on enemy computers. It operates under the 2nd Bureau of the GSD [People's Liberation Army General Staff Department, Third Department].

Prior to their arrival, the ODNI had communicated by its top secret methods with one Zhang Ling Min–a trusted employee of Apt 1 division of 61398—alerting him to an impending meeting with a high ranking U.S. Intelligence officer and to prepare a cover story to fit a visit to Shanghai East International Hospital at 150 Jimo Road, in Pudong. He had the perfect arrangement: his wife was in the late stages of her first pregnancy and needed to see her doctor for an "important visit".

Mr. Zhang had expected this event for several days. He called his wife to inform her that they were going to the hospital, to pack a bag, and to meet him at the door of their community residential complex. Lincoln watched Min walk out of the front door of the 12-story block building and over to the parking lot. They exchanged glances confirming that Min had recognized Lincoln's red pocket square.

The three went in separate cars: Sybil and Lincoln in a definitely used old Geely MK sedan that was once silver in color. Zhang Ling Min drove his company car, a gleaming new white Chery SUV, reserved for senior officials of the company. Min picked up his wife, and the three conspirators entered the hospital complex through separate entrances. Min dropped his wife off at the ob-gyn clinic with instructions that she be certain to obtain a certificate of attendance.

Sybil and Lincoln were sitting in the chapel donated by the Episcopalians with nearly full confidence that no one would interrupt them. Min entered, looked around; and seeing no one, walked quietly and sat one row behind the CIA agents.

Sybil and Lincoln greeted him as a friend.

Min looked several times at Sybil before saying, "Mrs. North, how you have aged. The last time we met, you were a chic modern forty-year-old Chinese fashion model."

Sybil and Lincoln laughed.

"Stresses of the job, Min. It takes its toll."

They spoke English, although all three were ready to switch to Mandarin immediately if a worshipper should appear.

"I know you do not have much time, Min; so, I will get right to the issue at hand. We are seeking a mass murderer who seems to be killing people indiscriminately around the world. The only real lead we have is a signature buried in the encrypted text that leads directly to APT 1. Frankly, the finding was a little too easy and obvious. Maybe, the killer—who calls himself 'Beelzebub'—is not as good with a computer as we first thought; or he made a mistake—everyone does occasionally—or he is purposefully including misinformation to throw us off. We need to track him...or her...or them...down before there are more massacres; and even worse, war between accusing nations."

Min maintained an Oriental inscrutable expression as most Chinese authorities did. But, he was obviously thinking.

"I think the misinformation option of the most likely. We, at APT 1 have been targeting American companies exclusively for the past six months. We are inside Wells Fargo, Chase Manhattan Bank, Trump Hotels, American Airlines…and, let's see…Boeing. Probably a few others, but that's all I know about for the time being. What I don't know is important. I have no knowledge of current attacks of governmental, defense, or medical entities. I have never heard of any misinformation mission to create chaos by pitting nations against each other in cyberspace. I, if anyone, should know of such secret intelligence initiatives."

Sybil had no good reason to doubt Min—his real name. He was born in Minneapolis, educated at UC Berkeley in computer science, and recruited by the CIA after he received and reported overtures from Chinese 61398 operatives. All of his information sent to the CIA and the ODNI had been rated A++, and he had never come under suspicion of being a double-agent.

"I know this will be touchy work, Min, and maybe dangerous. But, we need to know. Does anyone in the Third Department have any questionable communications with local or foreign entities that might be related to terrorism or to this Beelzebub character. It is only a matter of time before the Chinese, or the Russians, or the Islamists, or the Filipinos, launch a warning shot across the bow. I have influence with the Americans, of course; but I can't remain convincing much longer without objective evidence. I'm sure you know that there was a close call between the Filipinos and the PLA recently. The American DOD stepped in from behind the scenes and quieted things down. We have hawks in our military and in our intelligence services who are just waiting for an excuse."

"I will get my trusted people on it. It probably won't be easy. If the Chinese are involved, it will be very deeply hidden; so, I will have to dig deeply and be exposed to threat of being caught."

It was part of his job; so, he nodded, got up, and left the chapel.

"I take it you trust him, Sybil. You pretty much exposed our whole hand in that conversation," Lincoln said with genuine gravity.

"In this business, a lot depends on trust. Min and I have a strong mutual trust. Now, my friend, we must get to other areas of potential capable enemies. I am going to go from here to Moscow. I want you to head back to *Salar de Uyuni*. I have a hunch nagging at the back of my mind, that the incredibly valuable lithium market has something serious to do about this Beelzebub business. You need to dig deeply, mine everything possible from the electronic devices. I am sure there is a connection."

"Far be it from me to cast doubt on one of your famous hunches. I will give it my best. As my favorite detective would say, 'the game's afoot.'" [Lincoln knew the saying had originated with Shakespeare *King Henry IV Part I*, 1597, but he still liked to credit Sherlock Holmes.]

CHAPTER SEVEN

The secure telephone blinked red in FBI Director Landon Murphy's office. His aide, Emmanuel Dorrity, answered,

"This is a secure line. Tell me your clearance code, please," Emmanuel asked politely.

The answer was less polite, even brusque, "I speak to Landon and no one else. You will regret forever if you interfere."

"I will try and locate the director, Sir. Please stay on the line."

Emmanuel pushed the security button which activated a recording machine in the J. Edgar Hoover FBI building security office, and signaled officers to listen in on the call. Next, he called the director on his personal cell phone.

"This better be important."

"It may be, Sir. The voice is threatening, and I think it is more than just the usual crank call."

"A hunch?"

"I guess so; but, my gut is giving me a trouble signal"

"You usually have a good gut and good hunches. Are you ready for me to be patched in?"

"Yes, you will see the office number at the top of your screen. When you do, tap it; and you will be in direct contact with the caller."

"And I'll be recorded."

"Yes, officially."

Director Murphy watched his iPhone screen for a moment until the office number popped up. He took a breath and began to speak.

"This is FBI Director Landon Murphy speaking on the office secure line. Before we talk, give me your top-secret code and tell me how you came by this number."

"No, you boob. Listen to me. I have a message. I am the famous Beelzebub. Listen closely, I will not repeat myself. Instruct the treasury secretary to send forty billion dollars in gold bullion to the consulate in Paraguay addressed to me via the diplomatic pouch. I receive that gold in three days or China and Russia will be at war. Guaranteed. I am Beelzebub, the magnificent. Hark when I speak."

Just before the line went dead, there was a bone-chilling horror movie laugh, "hahaha."

Murphy learned that the call could not be traced, then, asked his aide to arrange a conference call among the presidents and heads of the US, Russia, China, the EU, the DCIA, the DNI, and DARPA.

In ten minutes, every leader had checked in, and the DFBI informed them of the threatening call.

President Willets spoke first, "I assure everyone on the line that the US had nothing to do with this and that we have been doing everything in our power to locate and to apprehend this Beelzebub character. If any of you are responsible for the sophisticated hacking; or, if your citizens have perpetrated the murderous atrocities committed in the name of this Beelzebub, now is the time to confess, be forgiven, and to help us all to get this person into custody or otherwise stopped. Nothing you could gain would be worth a Sino-Russian war which would soon spread everywhere."

President Willets was severely disappointed when his counterparts either refused to acknowledge their involvement, refused to talk about the subject—China and Russia—or laughed off the call and the Beelzebub story as a hoax or poppycock. It appeared that it was going to be the United States against Beelzebub alone.

First, they were going to have to find the monster. He had Norcroft, Murphy, Dr. Steven Highnam from DARPA, and Admiral Hyman Jincowitz, the DNI, remain on the line until all the leaders finished their sardonic laughs and their scoffing rejoinders and signed off.

"I think this is the real thing," President Willets said, "this Beelzebub jerk has never bluffed before, and no common crank caller could get access to the DFBI's phone like he or she or whatever did. We need some serious action. Something short of war, but serious."

Dr. Highnam spoke first, "This is a cyberattack until it becomes a physical attack, Mr. President. In my humble opinion, we need to execute a reversible, serious, attention getting preemptive strike to get their attention and to provoke real communication."

"Like Stutznet?" asked Dr. Highnam, Dr. Norcroft, and DFBI Murphy, almost simultaneously.

"Make it Stutznet on steroids," Murphy and Norcroft said, and smiled at the coincidence.

"My DARPA jokers can shut down the governments of the PRC and the Russian Federation, if you want."

"Reversibly?"

"Of course, Mr. President"

"And without wrecking our economy at the same time, Steven?" asked Sybil, looking directly into the man's eyes.

The look said that no one on the line would acquiesce to a half-baked disaster like the Stutznet attack on Iran that boomeranged.

"Guaranteed. We learned our lesson."

"How long will it take for you to put this new worm or virus into play, Dr. Highnam?" POTUS asked, "and how long will it take the rest of us to warn our own military and major industries and our real allies?"

There was a serious discussion. Finally, Sybil spoke for all the advisors to the president.

"We need a full day, and that's stretching it."

"Make it less," said POTUS.

There was as scramble to get the attacks ready and the warnings passed on. The question was, were they already too late?

CHAPTER EIGHT

They were too late. Beelzebub's organization put into action three separate matched attacks which they had pre-planned. The signal to begin was simply for the caller to the DFBI to hear the word, "no" to his outrageous demands. Simultaneously, the three attacks commenced.

The first was a pair of attacks, one against China, and the other against Russia. A Chinese submarine, *The Red Hunter*, sustained three hits from aerial launched self-propelled torpedoes with heavy explosive heads dropped into the sea from the undercarriage of the USSR fixed-wing double engine Tupelov-124 bomber. The old but reliable USSR aerial torpedoes were designed to explode when in close proximity to the submarine. All three bombs hit the target, and it dropped to the bottom of the South China Sea in less than five minutes. The markings from the exploded torpedoes found floating on the surface above the submarine resting in the deep clearly implicated Russia.

The paired attack against Russia occurred less than three seconds after the Chinese sub was hit. Ostensibly, several buildings at a secret military base–which manufactured and tested nuclear missiles in the small town of Nyonoska in Arkhangelsk region of far northern Russia—simultaneously blew to pieces by massive amounts of explosives. The explosives were CL-20 [20,2,4,6,8,10,12-hexanitro-2,4,6,8,10,12-hexaazaisowurtzitane ($C_6H_6N_{12}O_{12}$)], originally synthesized in 1986 at the Naval Surface Weapons Center at China Lake, California. CL-20 is the highest energy compound as well as the highest density compound known among organic chemicals. A warehouse burglary in 2018 at China Lake went unreported because of the top-secret clearance required even to admit to the possession of the dangerous material.

Late that afternoon, Norwegian authorities detected radioactive iodine in the waters near Arkhangelsk, thus confirming that Russia was making nuclear weapons there in that frozen wasteland. The following day, the US navy found debris clearly identified as belonging to the PLA [People's Liberation Army] The markings were in *pinyin: Zhōngguó Gōngnóng Hóngjūn*–Chinese Workers' and Peasants' Revolutionary Army. All debris was coated with residue of $C_6H_6N_{12}O_{12}$ which matched the batch stolen from China Lake. The implications were stunning enough, and reeked of cause to launch World War III, starting with China versus Russia and spreading throughout the "civilized" world. But, the second two pairs of shoes dropped within the United States behind the cloud of media blitz about the Chinese and Russian military attacks that quickly found its way into the public eye complete with fact checking from unknown sources.

The first pair of attacks occurring in the US included the dropping of a GBU-43B [US Massive Ordnance Air Blast–nicknamed the Mother Of All Bombs–a large-yield satellite-guided, air delivered bomb, described as the most powerful non-nuclear weapon in history] on an NAACP annual meeting held in the Dallas Cowboys Stadium [Jerry World] in Dallas. Besides the 100,000 people killed in the special events arrangement of the stadium that morning– as they listened to a replay of Martin Luther's famous "I have a dream" speech and a lecture by Clarence Thomas on cases pending in the Supreme Court on reparations for slavery and the crying need for more African-American, female, and LGBTQ-I judges and justices, there was insult added to the injury. An avalanche of vitriolic hate leaflets bearing scurrilous descriptions and drawings of African-American, Latino, and Jewish, people fluttered out of the smoky sky. The leaflets were signed: "White People Forever, all others, Never".

The mate to that pair of home-grown hate crimes against African-Americans occurred in Sterling, Virginia during a hot humid morning of an NRA weapons extravaganza. The true Second-Amendment aficionados were enjoying beer, corn-dogs, and an exposure to every kind of "defensive" weapon from Bowie knives to fully automatic submachine guns to Stinger missiles. The 97% Caucasian crowd listened to throbbing strains of white punk songs with metal-based accompaniment. Other genres included Nazi punk, Rock Against Communism, National Socialist black metal, old-time Gospel, and Modern Christian Rock music. Because of the wide spread publicity sponsored by the NRA and secretly by David Duke's KKK, the crowd was pumped up to hear a constitutional scholar's oration on their favorite amendment, and an appeal from the executive director of the NRA for more money to combat the looming threat by the dark-web and deep-state anti-gunners to confiscate their guns. There were nearly 250,000 highly patriotic, sunbaked, beer tranquilized, and Christian conservatives, on the grounds that morning. It was a great day.

It is doubtful if many of the 250,000 white party goers heard the impact of the three bunker buster bombs that dropped from the cloudless sunny skies and made huge craters in the crowded food concessions, weapons displays, and entertainment venues all gathering them around to entice the happy folks into their part of the narrowly drawn area. Within seconds, over 200,000 white Americans were dead, most of whom were obliterated or their body parts dumped helter-skelter into the enormous unnatural holes in the grassy fields. A veritable coalclinkerstorm of black leaflets emblazoned with white print littered the land and the bodies like falling dark autumn leaves. The message was simple: "How do y'all like them apples, Whitey?"

The final pair of atrocities launched on the same dreadful day took place in Mecca and at the Vatican. It was an important day of the annual hajj—the pilgrimage of faithful Muslims seeking to accomplish a once in a lifetime visit to the holy city—one of the five pillars of Islam and one of the most enjoyable of all experiences for the Believers. They were all there within view of the Kaaba—the "House of Allah", in the sacred city of Mecca in Saudi Arabia—during the Sacred Month of Dhul-Hijjah, the 12th month of Islamic calendar to participate in the seven steps of Hajj—all 1,800,000 of them. They were gathered around the Ka'aba walking slowly around the edifice counter-clockwise, many of the humbler souls enraptured with the experience. The murmur of the tightly compacted crowd was loud enough nearly to drown out the sound of two airplanes swooping overhead. The blue and white planes bore the unmistakable image of the Israeli flag.

The two large jet attack bombers—a Sukoi-Su 25, and a Dassault Étendard IV—hurtled towards the unsuspecting crowd of worshippers dropping thousands of "bombis" in three well-planned passes. The bomblets exploded in a blanketing of razor sharp and red-hot shards of steel cutting the victims to pieces. Early estimates were 820,000 dead, and another 200,000 critically wounded. The sacred stones of the plaza surrounding the Ka'aba were overrun by rivers of ankle-deep blood. The screams of the neglected wounded by the overwhelmed first-responders was too much even for seasoned soldiers and the smattering of terrorists attending to their religious duties. Grown men wept.

The survivors shrieked, "Death to the crusaders!"

To antagonize further the Muslim victims, leaflets in Arabic and Latin were found all over Mecca reading, "It is time for the Islamic terrorists to disappear. This is the first step!"

Finally—and at the same moment as all of the other major atrocities of the day—Vatican City was in the midst of a special event–a magnificent and holy event attended by every cardinal in the world, most of the archbishops and bishops, leaders of all of the monastic orders, and scores of Italian and world leaders, mostly those of a Roman Catholic persuasion. Nearly two million penitents and worshippers crowded Vatican square until fire marshals had to prohibit further entry. The streets around the square were soon filled to capacity, and the gendarmerie was hard put to maintain order. This was the annual August Feast of the Assumption, which is dedicated to the day Mary ascended into Heaven. There were no hotel rooms left, no bed and breakfasts, no camping spots, and no place for late comers or the poor to lay their heads the night before the 83-year-old 266th Pope, Francis appeared in the window of his apartment overlooking Saint Peter's Square. The crowd was so heavy that there was one group in the Audience Hall and another in St. Peters Basilica, and even filling the Barberini Gardens, to hear him. The bulk of the crowd staring upward from the square was a nearly monolithic sea of humanity.

Pope Francis intoned his Apostolic Blessing, then began his well-rehearsed Papal Audience. An apparently protective squadron of Italian air force light bombers streaked overhead. They made two passes wherein they dropped dozens of high explosive thermite incendiary bombs. More than a million of the faithful were enveloped and consumed in the resulting superheated fireball. The last plane dropped a cloud of leaflets which read, "Allah, the All-knowing and All-powerful has wrought His vengeance upon the kaffir nonbelievers and crusaders. Believe in Him or die!"

CHAPTER NINE

Secure telephones began to ring off their holders at 1700 hours that terrible day. Agents had to be brought into the main offices of the FBI, the CIA, and the ODNI, to handle the calls from vetted officers, diplomats, White House staffers, the DOD, and the DOJ. Calls from the public, news organizations, or other individuals or organizations lacking clearance for the "Beelzebub Case" were triaged to the round file (discarded after a polite digital "Thank you, and we will get back to you as soon as the volume of communication permits.")

President Willets ordered an emergency meeting in the Situation Room for 1730 hours with mandatory attendance by the VPOTUS, DCIA, DDCIA, DFBI, DDFBI, DNI, DDNI, the attorney general, cabinet secretaries [limited to Secretaries of State, Justice, Defense, Treasury, and Homeland Security], the entire JCOS, the director and deputy director of DARPA, Chief (and director) CH/CSS/DIRNSA [Central Security Service/ National Security Agency (DIRNSA), who also serves as (DirUSCYBERCOM) [Commander of the United States Cyber Command], DDNSA Cyber Command, and heads and deputy directors of every one of the seventeen intelligence services—including such little known agencies serving the intelligence community as the coast guard, the (NGA) [National Geospatial-Intelligence Agency], INR [United States Department of State Bureau of Intelligence and Research , and the TFI [United States Department of the Treasury Office of Terrorism and Financial Intelligence].

There were hawks and doves, diplomats and militarists, intelligence officers and analysts, all vying for the president's attention.

"You will all get your chance, but we are here to learn what information is available at this point about the Beelzebub person or entity, why he, she, or it, has done such terrible things to our world, and what we can do about it. I can tell you from my conversations with the Russians and Chinese, the Israelis and the Islamists, the ideologues all over this country pressing for one blood-letting or another that the world sits on the brink of a war that could dwarf even World War II. Right now, in this room, and with the cooperation of usually uncooperative foreign powers, we can either prevent war or achieve an uneasy truce. How long that can hold is unknown and controversial. I have been listening to you throughout the day and have every respect for your opinions. I tell you, for the sake of civilization and humanity, we will come up with a new idea in this meeting, or we will be witness to annihilation. The

DCIA has been on this since the day the first Beelzebub letter was sent to the *LA Times*; so, I want to hear from her first. Sybil, you have the floor."

"I won't waste your time. This is my take—my hunch, if you will. The attacks, terrible and costly as they have been, are phonies—contrived for the benefit of some individual or organization to achieve a nefarious purpose. I do not believe that we have seen bona fide military strikes by any country against another, or any ideology against another one. I do not have the authority to require any or all of you to step back and watch—to do anything other than to prepare for the worst. But, that is what I ask of you. Give the assembled intelligence services, working in conjunction with our real allies, the British, Israelis, and select Europeans, a chance to scour the earth for information, for evidence, and to be able to come up with a plan. I have some ideas I want to pursue.

"I fully recognize the gravity of the situation we face and how limited the time is. Do any of you remember the old Kingston Trio song, They're rioting in Africa?"

Several of the very grey heads nodded and smiled.

"The pertinent lyrics are:

…The whole world is festering with unhappy souls,

The French hate the Germans; the Germans hate Poles.

Italians hate the Yugoslavs; South Africans hate the Dutch.

…And I don't like anybody very much.

But we can be tranquil and thankful and proud

That man's been endowed with a mushroom-shaped cloud,
And we know for certain that some lovely day,
Someone will set the spark off,
And we will all be blown away."

"I might add—apropos of today—that it is not at all certain that the next 24 to 48 hours will determine if the Kingston Trio's lovely day will the one of the next two. I will go to Moscow tonight to track down some likely suspects. My main agent is in Beijing as we speak. Our colleagues in the FBI are in the air and headed to the Philippines and to Riyadh. Other agents are already in New Martinsville, West Virginia and in Jamaica Plains, the Bronx, New York City. The investigation service of the State Department has volunteered to visit the Vatican, the Gaza Strip, and the Syrian Idlib governate. We can't get to all the haters, but those will be a good start.

"I have to say that some serious and well-placed somebody somewhere has a severe axe to grind. We have to find him or her.

"Finally, the DOJ and Homeland Security have their own lists of haters to chat with. The DOD is busy preparing for Armageddon. That should keep us all busy for the next day or so. Does anyone else have a nonpartisan suggestion about where there is a stone to turn over?"

Not surprisingly, the democrats in the room suggested hotbed cities of the alt-right or high voter turn-out for the republicans—Mesa, Arizona and Oklahoma City,

Oklahoma. The Republicans targeted San Francisco and Boulder, Colorado.

POTUS ordered everyone to keep away from reporters of any stripe and to report back to the White House as the information clearing center.

His final exhortation was, "Go with God my friends. We have a world and a civilization to save."

VPOTUS stood beside President Willets and put both hands in the air with V for Victory signs.

CHAPTER TEN

Bad news continued to flow in at an accelerated rate. A-P news services reported that Boeing, Airbus Group, Lockheed Martin, Raytheon, and General Atomics, had been targeted. A-P said that it was as yet unclear what had been stolen; but DARPA and the intelligences services cyber units knew that millions of secure addresses, schematics, and plans, had been compromised by China. Lincoln Howard reported the work of Zhang Ling Min—a trusted employee of Apt 1 division of 61398, the Chinese government hacking service–and his own contribution as a spy for Sybil. The DCIA was—at the moment—in a Russian made turboprop Antonov AH-32 transport plane flying over the North Atlantic en route to Moscow.

Sybil listened intently to Lincoln's report that was considered too sensitive to transmit in writing. She was seated in a comfortable leather-bound reclining swivel chair and wearing head-phones for privacy. Her plane was supplied by Air Branch–the aviation wing of SAD [the

CIA's Special Activities Division]. The airplane had been modified by the division for covert missions in support of CIA operations. She had been trying to rest during the >2,000 mile air trip when Lincoln called.

"Sorry it took so long to get through security this time, Lincoln. What do you have to report?"

"We have pinpointed the hackers who got into our aircraft manufacturing companies. They are a Russian cyberespionage group—known as "Fancy Bears". They collude with the Chinese 61398. We have names and even know which computers in the building off Datong Road in the public, mixed-use area of Pudong in Shanghai with which you are thoroughly familiar."

"The same building—known to every intelligence organization in the developed world—which houses PLA Unit 61398/APT 1? That Pudong building?"

"The very same. Our Chinese and Russian friends are up to their ears in this Beelzebub business. Why, is not entirely clear."

"Maybe it is just grand theft on a colossal scale; DARPA tells me that Beelzebub has now frozen whole computer operations in these companies temporarily with ransom ware. Someone needs to get on the line with the kidnapped companies and plead with them not to pay ransom. We estimate that more than sixty billion dollars has been paid out for ransom already," Sybil told Lincoln.

"It's more than just money, Sybil. We have learned that a group called the Honker Union has political motives. The group formed when the United States bombed the Chinese embassy in Belgrade, Yugoslavia. So-called Honkers formed a Honker Union, whose members combined hacking skills with misplaced patriotism and nationalism, and launched a series of attacks on websites in the United States, mostly government-related sites. The group uses the communist party red color to distinguish itself. They romanticize their activities with the idea that a hacker in red is in combat with evil hackers in the dark. Eventually Honkers morphed their hacktivism to support the Chinese government against what they see as the imperialism of the United States and the militarism of Japan. Last year, the group merged with the Red Hacker Alliance."

Sybil replied, "And, I'm beginning to think this whole affair is a very complicated set of actions, and we don't really know the core reason for all of this theft and mayhem. Lincoln, I have a theory that we have a mole working against us—and by us, I mean the whole civilized world—for his or her own gain. I am on my way to Russia to feel the government out about cooperating instead of fighting with the Chinese and eventually us. I may be wrong, but I am pretty sure that greed and a play for power underlie this terrible calamity that has been developed on purpose."

"So, you don't think Beelzebub, or Satan, or the Prince of the Knight, the Dark Force, or the Deep Space is behind all of this devilish business, eh, Sybil?"

"And I don't believe in spirits, ghosts, or fairy dust, Lincoln. In the end, I think we will find some power mad person or group who has come up with an incredibly successful way to garner money for the cause. The world has lost over a trillion dollars up to know, with three-quarters of that being money that is gone over to the dark side to support the monsters' purposes."

"Would it be a good idea to have the DDCIA meet with his counterpart in Beijing and try to spread the idea you have? We are all going to agree, or a great many of us are going to die."

"That's a good idea. While we're at it, I'll work on President Willets to send emissaries to the Japanese, Russian, Saudi, Israeli, and Palestinian, governments to convince them to back off from military belligerence until we know what is really going on."

"I'll keep working here in China, Sybil. The only real set of facts we have for sure right now is that 61398 is involved. I want to see if Min and I can develop some leads that implicate some big snootin' grouper in one of our countries as the culprit."

"That is exactly my plan for going to Moscow. Check in with me tomorrow night, if you can, Lincoln. Let's pool every resource and bit of information. Stay safe, my friend."

The turboprop Antonov AH-32 landed in near total darkness at the Moscow Domodedovo Airport, the large, busy, domestic facility that the CIA deemed safer for the security of the DCIA and her mission.

She was whisked aboard a re-worked unobtrusive 2105 Classic Lada–originally a knock-off, based on the 1966 Fiat 124. The Lada sedan was the most common model and was most appreciated for its affordable price, its reliability, and the unpretentious mechanics. The American spies appreciated the current American revised version which looked beat-up and no better or no more worthy of a glance the other several million of them still on Russian streets.

Sybil slid onto the spacious seat's leather comfort and met Special Agent, Danny Mortensen, with whom she had worked in the jungles of the Congo four years previously.

There was not enough time to indulge in doubt and suspicion. She came right to the point.

"Danny, tell me what you know."

"Yes, Madam Director. I do know this much. There has been a great deal of money flowing into the side doors of the Lubyanka FSB building. I'm not sure the head of the Federal Security Service knows whether, how much, or for what purposes. Even stranger, my people have spotted some known faces from the APL-1 in Shanghai, from the Honker Union, from the Islamic State, Israel, and from the Fatah."

"Sounds like dinner with the Satan family."

"Yeah, it does. What do you think is up, Director?"

She told Danny what she knew and what she surmised.

"A mole? Think it could be an American mole, even a CIA mole?"

"Heaven forbid; but no one is above or beyond suspicion, Danny, not even me."

The driver of the Russian car had been told simply to drive around and await more definitive orders.

"What's your plan, Madam Director?"

"I need you to take me to the basement of the Lubyanka, Danny. Time is very short, and I need to scare the crap out of some teenagers."

"Putin's own teenage hackers?"

"Yes, unless, you have a better target of my inquiries."

"I am out of ideas. But, Director, did you know that the Lubyanka is considered the tallest building in Russia?"

"No, I didn't. I don't. How can that be true?"

"Because, as it is said, 'from the basement of the Lubyanka, you can see Siberia a thousand miles away.'"

She offered Danny a sardonic smile.

The clever and pampered "princes of the internet", led cloistered and sheltered lives, and also viewed their very secure lives as being slaves to the machinery of the Lubyanka and its denizens. The teenagers Sybil needed to meet worked from Pb [*informatsionnoye protivoborstvo* or Information countermeasures]. She would need the permission of Alexander Bortnikov, head of the FSS [Federal Security Service] who reported directly to President Vladimir Putin.

"It would probably be better to see Alexander Bortnikov first," Danny suggested. "I doubt you will get past the main doors without a pass from him."

"I don't think that will be a problem. He and I worked together about ten years ago on a human trafficking case. We seemed to hit it off."

It turned out that Sybil was right. Borntikov opened his schedule to fit her in as soon as he knew she was in the city and was requesting help. The Russian government was in enough of a panic to be willing to talk to any senior US officer to help avoid a massive escalation in hostilities in the Middle East. And, he liked Sybil Norton, ever since she adroitly rebuffed his overly enthusiastic advances in a time long ago and far away, as he saw it.

She entered a rear door into the Lubyanka and was quickly escorted to Bortnikov's large and ornate office.

"Sybil, my dear, it has been such a long time," he said. "How good it is to see you. We are all very worried at these uncertain times. Is there a way we can all help each other?"

"I certainly hope so, Sasha," she said, using his familiar nickname. "I have come with a mission. You and I must be honest with each other; I promise that on my end. The stakes are too high for any pretenses."

"I agree. At first, here, we all thought the Chinese had gone crazy, which is not at all like them. Then, we decided it was a plot by the Americans to take back the prestige they once enjoyed in Asia before the yellow-haired man became the 'little Tzar' as we called him. It was a trick to get us and the Chinese to tear at each other's throats. I held out against that idea. We have not been on good terms with your government, but I never believed the thoughtful people like you in the American government would hatch such a scheme. It would eventually result in terrible harm to your citizens as well as the rest of the world."

"Sasha, I have been running around like a chicken with its head cut off trying to find out who or what this Beelzebub character is and why he or it is working so disastrously to cause dissension. You are right about us. President Willets is not crazy, and neither am I. I have my finger on the pulse of everything our country is doing with regards foreigners. Categorically, I can say it is not us who are the monsters. Frankly, I don't think it is the Chinese either. As you say, it is not in their nature. They are long-term planners, and this Beelzebub thing is the quintessence of short-term disaster."

"Do you have one of your famous hunches, my dear? I presume you are here–and in a hurry–to keep the planet from being blown away by the hawks in America, Russia, China, and the Middle East."

"I have something of an idea. It is only partial, and I know it is neither the whole story nor the solution. However, I think your cyber counterintelligence bureaus may hold the answer or can help me to find it. I need your permission. The Politburo and the Chairman may well not like it, but I have to have some serious access."

"That's a big ask, my friend, especially with everything so tense right now. However, I trust you. If I am wrong, and you betray me; it will cost me my life. I will clear the way for you. Please, by all you hold dear, do not use this clearance to trick me."

He was intensely serious, even emotional, a characteristic Sybil would never have thought the man of iron could possess.

"You have my word, Sasha. All of our lives may depend on our trust of each other."

"So, what do you want, specifically?"

"I need to have full and unimpeded access to your Information Countermeasures Group—the adolescent hackers who are so brilliant and resourceful."

"You have met them before and jousted with them, as I recall."

"I did. That was an unfortunate time when the *russkaya mafiya* launched an attack on our stock markets. That is all in the past. Bad as that was, this situation is far worse."

"I will take you to them this very day."

When an FSB limousine races through Moscow, just as happened when it was the KGB, pedestrians and vehicles scurried to get out of the way and did not ask questions.

The house where the young hackers worked was large but unimpressive, very much like all the rest of the Khrushchev concrete block buildings on the street. There was no impressive show of security, but Sybil knew it was one of the most closely guarded secrets in the Russian Federation and secured as such.

She and Director Borntikov moved swiftly through a side door and up two flights of stairs. The entire floor was dedicated to the tasks of a group of twenty young Russian boys and girls. They looked like any other gathering of millennials—crazy haircuts and colors, tattoos all over, and a number of rings and ear lobe guagers–including straight and curved ear stretching tapers and claws for making ever larger holes in their earlobes—all where such things should not be, in Sybil's opinion. Their clothing was like that of youth all over the world—torn knees, mixed and mis-matched colors, sizes, styles, and mostly immodest enough to compel Sybil to fix her eyes on the eyes of the boys and girls.

Sybil knew not to under-estimate these pampered children. Because of their level of computer genius, they had been imported from all over the Russian Federation to engage in cyberwarfare for the Russian government. This included denial of service attacks, hacker attacks, dissemination of disinformation and propaganda, participation of state-sponsored teams in political blogs, internet surveillance using SORM technology [System for Operative Investigative Activities], persecution of cyber-dissidents, and other even more active measures.

Sybil wanted to make use of their combined skills and knew she had to win them over. Moreover, she was determined to get them to work with the Chinese Honker Union, their counterparts in the Peoples' Republic.

Their director introduced Sybil to the assembled hackers and smilingly asked them to give every help they could to this American spy master. There was no point in being coy or secretive about her identity. They all knew perfectly well who Sybil Norcroft was and regarded her as an enemy agent. It was her mission to win them over and to do so quickly.

"Thank you all for taking time away from your important work. The world is in a serious state of threat as you all know. Much of the threat has originated from black hat hacking. I am pretty sure that some of you have been assigned to do some of that work; in fact that you have linkages with the Fancy Bears who work with the Chinese Red Honkers. Well, I can say without reservation, that you and the other hackers around the world have succeeded beyond your wildest imaginations—which are pretty wild, I am told."

She was gratified to see that she had elicited a little laughter around the room.

"Look, Director Borntikov and I–and in fact, the whole world–needs your help and needs it quickly. That is no exaggeration. I have a daughter named Cerisse, who is also a great hacker. You may know about her."

They all nodded. Everyone in the room had heard the harrowing story of the little pygmy girl who was abused in the Congo, escaped by the heroism of her adoptive mother, and who was kidnapped and held for ransom— another story of great resourcefulness and bravery.

"I have traveled to the ends of the earth for her, for you, and for the young people growing up now; so, they can enjoy funny hairdos, tattoos, piercings and poor choices in clothing styles."

Now, the room rocked with laughter. Sybil knew she had them.

Sybil did not realize how extensive the hackers were involved themselves, but they were fickle and responded to the highest bidder, which—at the moment—was Sybil Norcroft and her old friend, Alexander Borntikov. It was only a matter of minutes before the room's computer keyboards were buzzing with activity—some redoing their previous hacking, some hacking new targets, and some doing creative detective work with a few gentle nudges from the two directors.

CHAPTER ELEVEN

The first break in the computer hacking room of the Lubyanka came just before midnight. Everyone in the room was exhausted, and their nerves were frayed. Michael Yvgenevich Petrovsky had been working all day on a hunch he had about the Chinese involvement in the vast hacking operation. First, he had put in several hours trying to connect to the Irans Quds military counter-intelligence actions over the last month. He found no connection to the Chinese, the Russians, or Islamic terrorist organizations. Michael decided that he had come to a dead-end and was about to give up. Then the answer was handed to him in a moment of illuminating serendipity.

He decided to check incoming e-mail messages from the United States to the *russkiya mafiya*. He was tired and looking into Russia's premier ongoing criminal enterprise was about as likely to turn up valuable evidence as writing a letter to Father Christmas at the North Pole. But, Michael was trained to look for small things, nuances. He found an encrypted set of e-mails going to and from the US Navy, the Chinese Honker Union, and the *vory v zakone* [syndicate boss and chief of the "thieves-in-law" of the *Solntsevskaya Bratva*] and the *russkiya mafiya*. Never before had he or anyone else run across any communication by the US military to the lords of crime in the Russian Federation. That in and of itself was enough to cause a spike in his epinephrine blood level. But there was something else: something small, nuanced, and something that would likely have been overlooked by a lesser hacker. It appeared in the middle of a long stretch of 0s and 1s, 1s and 0s. Michael deciphered tiny fragments that clearly decrypted as "Beelzebub the Magnificent", "orders from BtheM", and a sentence that included a reference that read, "payment in full for work done" which was signed BtheM, followed by a bewildering translation of "Ha, ha, ha."

Michael had had profitable and uncomfortable computer business—hacking business—with the Russian "Godfather" but had never run across anything like this. He had never heard of Beelzebub, the Magnificent, before the first A-P service news came out with their online, pre-print, reference to the American/European devil figure. He ran to Director Bortnikov and DCIA Norcroft with his finding.

The directors immediately realized they were on to something significant.

Bortnikov gave Michael Yvgenevich a direct order, "Dig deeper. Find something else in those e-mails. I am going to put a tap on the *vory v zakones* phone and all his communications. At this point I need to discuss the matter with President Putin, and I expect Director Norcroft to connect with President Willets. Good work. Now get some helper bees and find something we can work with."

Half a dozen of the best hackers and cybercounter intelligence officers began to work feverishly. At 0200, Michael reported back.

"Directors, we have found only one other rather strange thing. There are multiple encrypted messages to and from and about "geniuses" working with linguistics. I looked up what an arcane study of foreign languages had to do with our area of interest. I am not exactly sure what is going on; but one thing is clear, the volume of communications among all our suspects is not at all ordinary. They are deeply involved with each other. Even the decrypted messages are spoken of in some sort of personal messaging code. The most common communicator is the US Navy, and many of the messages come from a computer in a naval facility referred to only as the U.S. Naval Observatory in Washington, D.C.

"Are you absolutely sure, Michael?" asked an obviously upset Sybil Norcroft.

"Absolutely, Director. We have found the street address for the naval observatory, which is Number 1 Observatory Circle, U.S. Naval Observatory, Washington, D.C. Its GPS coordinates are 38.9230°N 77.0654°W."

Sybil turned pale, "Excuse me, Gentlemen, I have to contact my president again. In the meantime, Michael, find everything you can about linguistics and language study, especially the IP addresses used in the conversations you found."

Michael nodded. Bortnikov smiled. And Sybil gritted her teeth.

Sybil left the room and stepped outside the building to enhance her chances of having a secure conversation with POTUS.

President Willets' Oval Office secretary took the call.

"This is a secure line. Give me your credentials and clearance code."

Sybil did so, and repeated her clearance: Top Secret TS/SCI code clearance, with access to sensitive compartmentalized information and "need-to-know" status

"And you need to talk to POTUS?"

"Immediately."

"Is it an emergency?"

"Most definitely."

The next voice Sybil heard was that of the president.

"I presume this is not a social call or one to convey good news, Sybil. What do you have?"

"The Russians have found the source—the center—of digital communication with and for Beelzebub."

"That's bad news all by itself."

"It gets worse. The IP address has been traced to a single computer located in the basement of the Naval Observatory in Washington, D.C."

"Merciful heaven...the residence of the vice president of the United States...that naval observatory?"

"Yes, Mr. President–checked, rechecked, and confirmed. There is not a scintilla of doubt about that. Of course, at this point, we do not know who has been using the computer in the residence of VPOTUS."

"As soon as we ring off, I will put into action a complete surveillance on VPOTUS and all of his communications. I will restrict his access. It will take a little doing not to spook him. The FBI will take charge of the investigation. You can step back away from him for now. You continue to monitor and to chase down the people he communicates with. Any indication of a relationship with our favorite public enemy number one?"

"We have. It's skimpy for now; not enough to indict; but we have the best crooks in the world working on it. One oddity–besides seeing Beelzebub's encrypted name–is the presence of oblique references to 'linguistics'. Apparently, that is something different from language study. News at eleven, Mr. President."

"This goes no further than those of use with 'need-to-know'. It may be that the public will never learn about it. I can't think of any greater blow than to learn that the number two officer in the United States is a monster."

Michael Yvgenevich Petrovsky and his six co-horts worked through the night, partnering with their counterparts in DARPA and the FBI CRRU [Cryptanalysis and Racketeering Records Unit], and the Cyber Division's Investigative Department. The implications, even beyond this specific case, were appreciated immediately: computer intrusion cases—counterterrorism, counterintelligence, and criminal—are cyber program priorities because of their potential national security nexus. Everyone recognized the dual needs for an all-out effort to unearth any pertinent evidence and to let the chips fall where they may. They also committed to an absolute pact of secrecy with only a small handful of vetted officers knowing the whole story…ever.

General information about the scholastic and pragmatic field of linguistics came in fairly quickly since it was public knowledge and a field of masters and doctoral study in several major universities. The white hat hackers (as of the moment) assembled a comprehensive list of institutions around the world with recognized applied linguistics while Sybil and Alexander Bortnikov worked through the night to pare down the list to a workable few.

Although a large number of localities had been attacked by Beelzebub, the main countries targeted had been the US, Russia, the PRC, and England. They reasoned that Beelzebub—with all his delusions of grandiosity—would seek to work with and through major centers of applied linguistics education and companies that specialized in the use of that science commercially. They further limited the choices to areas that more digital traffic was being uncovered. Therefore, the first list included: the University of West Virginia in Morgantown; Stanford University in Stanford, California; Yale University in New Haven, Connecticut; Harvard University in Cambridge, Massachusetts; University of Florida, in Gainesville, Florida; and NYU in New York City.

Outside the US, they narrowed the list of universities to Oxford and Cambridge in England; the Sorbonne, in Paris; the University of Bonn, Germany's Center for European Integration Studies (ZEI) which provides future oriented research on unresolved issues of European integration and the global role of Europe, especially including a world recognized applied linguistics department; the American University in Cairo and Cairo University; Iran University of Science and Technology; King Abdulaziz University, in Jeddah, Saudi Arabia; United Arab Emirates University, Al Ein, UAE; and–following a Sybil hunch–Damascus University in Damascus, Syria.

The already overburdened hackers took a short nap then began the Herculean task of hacking the linguistics departments of every university on the short list; they accepted help from DARPA, INSCOM [the US Army Intelligence and Security Command], DCHC [DIA's Defense Counterintelligence and Human Intelligence Center], DS/ICI/CI [US Diplomatic Security Service U.S. Department of State], ONCIX [Office of the National Counterintelligence Executive], and the Chinese Honkers—whom nobody trusted; so, their tasks were limited to nonsensitive questions.

A small army of intelligence agents from the pertinent US agencies, including the FBI, US-CERT [the US Computer Emergency Readiness Team] and the trusted British CERT-UK began an emergency collaboration on computer network defense involving the designated universities and companies and agreed to share everything learned to address the cyber threats and manage cyber incidents encountered as necessary. This collaboration brought in GCHQ [United Kingdom Government Communications Headquarters], and MI5 [Security Service].

Sybil preferred to work with Humint intelligence activities because it suited her penchant for following her hunches. She made a series of brief secure calls:

To Cairo SAC—"this is a secure line. No names. You recognize my voice. Drop everything else and get to the head of the department of applied linguistics at the American University. The questions are: Do you know or know of Beelzebub? Do you or your department do any business of any kind with anyone in the present American administration? Do you have links to the Muslim Brotherhood, and do they have links to Beelzebub: Money is no object. Play nice unless they balk, then do what must be done. Out."

To Damascus SAC—"This a secure top-secret communication. Need anything ASAP about communications of government and intelligence officials regarding a person or organization named Beelzebub. Visit head of Damascus University Department of Applied Linguistics. Need anything about communication, business, or advising same person. You have covert links to AQI, AI, and an assortment of similar sorts of people. Call in your markers and do it quickly. Out."

To Gainesville SAC FBI— "Per DFBI this is top-secret secure communication. Need all info on applied linguistics transmissions between or involving a person or entity called Beelzebub. Anything about business, confidential or personal communications, etc. Money is no object. Out."

To Morgantown Chief of Police—"Hello, Chief. I hope you recognize my voice. Please, no names. We are tracking Beelzebub and need your help. Please get to University of West Virginia Department of Applied Linguistics and learn everything you can as fast as you can. Get back to me ASAP, even if the news is negative. Thanks."

After a two-hour power nap, Sybil herself met her pilot at the Moscow Domodedovo Airport and boarded the turboprop Antonov AH-32 to begin a whirlwind personal quest.

CHAPTER TWELVE

S top One: Jeddah, Saudi Arabia. Sybil was met by Special Agent Hank Desmond who transported her to the Department of Linguistics, King Abdulaziz University, where they met Khalid bin Ali Al Humaidan, the Director General of GIP [General Intelligence Presidency/*Al Mukhabarat Al A'amah*], Prince Abdullah Hussein ibn Saud, President of the University, and Dr. Fahd bin Nayef, head of the department.

Frankly, Sybil did not hold out much hope of getting good intelligence from the usually secretive and paranoid Saudis, but she was surprised.

"Please have a seat, Director," Al Humaidan offered. "We have been hard at work to find out the information you called about, and I think we have a line on your quarry."

"Thank you, Director General, I am on a fishing expedition, as you know; and it will be a relief to catch something right off the bat. Please cut to the chase."

"I love your American expressions like, 'cut to the chase,' they hit the target rather nicely. Here is a copy of four e-mails sent to the deputy director of the linguistics department. To use the common expression, we 'hacked' his private e-mails."

He handed her the four documents. The IP address was from the Naval Observatory in DC. That was corroborating, but also somewhat disappointing. The sender was naval Lieutenant Samuel Richard Tosker—of whom Sybil had never heard anything before. The recipient was BtM@AOL.com and the electronic signature was Ha ha ha. The text was about how applied linguistics worked as a science in the first two e-mails. The third and fourth e-mails discussed back and forth about setting up a Saudi corporation in Sana'a, Yemen to be named Saudi Professional Applied Linguistics, Ltd. The most gaping absence was the lack of any other named individual. The most telling sentence in the four e-mails was "You have the funding; I have the expertise and the experts. We can control communications in every nation that speaks English, Mandarin, Arabic, and Russian, for a start. What we need for the next three months is a little more good chaos." Signed Little BtM Ha ha ha.

"Do you know the location of these people, Director?"

"Oh, but of course. Sybil, you know from personal experience the effectiveness of *Al Mukhabarat Al A'amah.*"

She did indeed, and it made her shudder inwardly, an emotion she kept to herself by maintaining a soda-cracker facial expression.

"Care to share?"

"Anything to oblige our good American friends."

"*Said the crocodile to the scorpion on his back,*" thought Sybil.

"I need to have a quick talk with Lt. Tosker, please, Sir."

"We thought perchance that you would like to do that. We fashioned an emergency message to the very interested lieutenant, and he arrived in Jeddah last night. In fact, he is now sitting in Dr. Fahd bin Nayef's inner office awaiting the Devil Himself."

"Is he feeling well?"

"Whatever could you be suggesting, Sybil? He is, in fact, having a fine old time chatting with a truly brilliant young graduate student about applied linguistics, which is her chosen PhD field. Oh, did I mention that the young lady is not only very bright; she is a truly stunning beauty?"

"One of yours, Director?" Sybil asked with a knowing smile.

"Of course, My Friend; it would be lax of me to have it otherwise."

Sybil had no time for chit-chat or for romancing the lieutenant when she came to face him.

"Lieutenant, do you recognize me?"

"I'm sorry, Ma'am, you look familiar, but I can't place you."

"My name is Sybil Norcroft. I am the current director of the United States Central Intelligence Agency. I am here on a mission ordered by the president of the United States. I am busy, and I am serious. I have a few questions. If you value what is left of your pathetic little life, you will answer me truthfully and promptly."

Without glancing at the document handed her by CIA Saudi Arabia SAC Hank Desmond, she rattled off in fast precise English the family names, ages, general histories, present locations, and even the names of pets of Lt. Tosker's nuclear family—eight people in all, the youngest age two–and of his parents, his wife's parents, and all six of their siblings. She made not threats, not even a harsh look—just business.

Lt. Tosker was not a stupid man. He knew he had been threatened by an expert, and that she was capable of carrying out any threat he could even imagine.

He paused for only a moment, "What do you want to know, and what kind of deal can I get? Immunity?, Witsec? Guaranteed safety for my family? I know quite a lot; not everything; but enough to get me killed by this Beelzebub dude, if it ever gets out that I ratted."

"Lieutenant, recognize that I have all the leverage and that you are, as of this moment, a guest of the Saudi Arabian government. That could be permanent, brief, or very, very long. The rest of your...suggestions...depend on what you tell me that I can use in a court. That court may not be one that gets public scrutiny, mind you; but it still likes to have real evidence. Start talking."

He began slowly and haltingly; but after a minute, the wind got into his sails; and he poured out volumes of detailed information.

"What I know for a fact is that the whole Beelzebub enterprise is a very complex and interwoven network. I doubt that anyone but the man or woman who heads the thing actually knows the leader or the names of the leadership group. They have a massive amount of money collected from ransomware, extortion of governments and big companies, and from small cities, and cybertheft. To keep the victims of extortion willing to pay the exact amount demanded, the leadership has been scrupulous about keeping its promises. Once you pay, we leave you alone. China, Russia, England, and the US, have so far refused to give in. That means more terroristic attacks in those countries.

"I can give you the bank—it's in Lichtenstein—that paid me my two million bucks. But, I don't know any names other than that of the clerk that signed the check. I know the person who gives me orders—name of Gordon Lang, who works in the Agriculture Department. I know the person to whom I give information and instructions—name is Olivia Packer, works for Siemens. I know they're important because this Packer woman is a director in the Siemens department involved in cybersecurity, including: infrastructure, digital transformation charge, applied linguistics, automation, digitalization, and electrification."

The confession was recorded; and as soon as pertinent information was revealed, Sybil sent it along to the intelligence services and cybersecurity units of the relevant companies and nations. It took an hour to extract every bit of information the man had.

Sybil looked at Lt. Tosker when he sagged back in his chair and said, "I have just sent a message to the FBI to pick up your family and to take them to Fort Meade,

Maryland to keep them safe. You are going to be taken to the brig in the same secure location, but you will not be allowed to speak to your family. That is as far as I will go. You are a traitor on the highest level. You should be executed but be grateful that the worst that happens to you is that you stay healthy alone in living quarters the size of your master bedroom closet for the rest of your life."

She walked away and boarded her plane bound for Munich for a meeting with Olga Gabler, head of BSI [*Bundesamt für Sicherheit in der Informationstechnik*—the upper-level federal agency in charge of managing computer and communication security for the *German* government]. It is the German Federal Office for Information Security, digital counterintelligence, and cyber security]; Heinrich Wolfgang Streble, head of the BND [*Bundesnachrichtendienst* Federal foreign intelligence and security service; Deiter Langerter, chief of the BKA [*Bundeskriminalamt*—Federal criminal intelligence and security service]; and Lieutenant General Pieter Sturmgarten III, the head of MAD [*Amt für den Militärischen Abschirmdienst*—Federal military intelligence and security service].

She had prearranged the meeting and its purpose: a federal raid on the *Aktiengesellschaft* [Siemens AG] cybersecurity and digitalization unit located on Werner-von-Siemens-Straße in Munich. Shortly before landing she was informed that Siemens CEO, Joe Kaeser, had agreed not to challenge the raid and to secure full cooperation in return for keeping the raid and its purpose out of the news media. He would be joining the senior intelligence officers during the raid.

Sybil and her entourage of important intelligence officials, the CEO, and a German signals and cybersecurity expert, swept quickly through the large building and up to the third floor. Joseph Finklestein—the director the cyber and digitalization unit—was sitting in his plush office working diligently on his computer when the entourage marched into his office and gave him the scare of his life.

"*Was ist die Bedeutung dieser?*" Finklestein demanded in a trembling voice.

CEO Kaeser said, "Do not be alarmed, Joseph, the meaning of this is that a Siemens employee or more than one may be implicated in the heinous Beelzebub case. These people are scouring the world for any information that would bring the criminals to justice and to put a stop to this senseless killing. You are requested to cooperate."

Finklestein knew full well what a "suggestion" from Joe Kaeser meant.

He calmed down and said, "What can I do to help?"

"First, and very quietly, we need to know the exact location of your co-worker, Olivia Packer. Second, these agents will bring in a small army of specialists to take over every computer in your division. You are to give the order, and to tell them to lift their hands above their heads and away from their keyboards immediately. They will share every password they have, even personal ones. *Verstehen sie?*"

Finklestein answered meekly, "*Ja, Ich verstehe.*"

"He understands and will cooperate fully," Kaesar told Sybil and the entourage.

With one exception, the computer searches and personal interrogations went with smooth German efficiency. That exception was a mousy mustachioed little man named Luis B. Cappachio, who made a mad dash for the exit, dropping his papers, his computer mouse, and his brief case, on the floor as he ran. The signals and cybersecurity expert tackled Luis; and, in short order, he and Olivia Packer were ensconced in the Siemens security office under armed guard.

Sybil and the German intelligence leaders began a hard and detailed interrogation of the pair after explaining the potential consequences of lying or obfuscating to questions posed in a national security emergency.

Packer and Cappachio feared the murky unknown figure they knew only as Beelzebub the Magnificent; but, for the moment, they feared the American and German intelligence officers more. They admitted working together to further the Beelzebub enterprise for the staggering sum of 3.6 million € [4 million USD] each. Their families were promised by Sybil and her co-horts lifetime security, and they were promised that they would not be extradited or executed. For that largesse, they spilled their guts.

The following pertinent things were learned: the pair had facilitated in Siemens' name the laundering of nearly a trillion USD through a consortium of banks regularly used by terrorists. Their unsuspecting co-workers—who believed they were working for the German government—had set aside their real work and had begun hacking major governmental and company computer secrets and transmitting them to a private computer center in Morgantown, West Virginia in the US. Unknown to the CEO of Siemens, the company gave its stamp of approval to the use of its digital technology, expertise, and machinery, to cause the Chinese and Russian attacks on each other.

That piece of information alone put to rest any further antagonisms between the two nations, and the rest of the world who were made privy to the information were relieved of a huge angst. Immediately after walking out of the Siemens' headquarters building, Sybil called Lincoln Howard on his sat phone and told him to go to Morgantown and why. She boarded her plane for the same destination. There seemed to be some clearing of the fog of deception, but Sybil was far from satisfied.

CHAPTER THIRTEEN

Despite the longer distance by air, Lincoln reached Morgantown, West Virginia half a day sooner than Sybil. By the time they met, Lincoln had rounded up the local FBI CIRG [Critical Incident *Response Group*] agents, Morgantown SWAT, and the West Virginia state highway patrol Special Response Team. They were suited up in their game day uniforms with all security precautions and were waiting impatiently to converge on the Morgantown Applied Linguistics and Media Development Center, a private company about which the local police could not find out very little.

Sybil's driver parked half a block away from where the law enforcement agents and officers had gathered. She was outfitted and armed the same as the rest of the agents in keeping with her basic credo of "A working woman, I am, and tried and true. I wouldn't ask you nothin' I wouldn't do."

It was obviously no coincidence that a letter signed Lincoln introduced her all around. None of the men or the two women thought to suggest that this attractive slender woman should be held back in a protective rear guard.

"Thank you, Lincoln. Could you all give me the current sitrep?"

Lincoln and Lt. Col. Hershey Watson, head of the state patrol response unit brought her up to speed in short clipped and pertinent sentences—no long descriptions, and no lengthy opinions.

"Who is in tactical charge?"

"I am presuming that you are in overall strategic command, Madam DCIA; and with your consent, I will take tactical command," Col. Watson told her.

She nodded her agreement and said, "Let's do this."

Per the prearranged plan agreed to by all units, the separate organizations advanced on the rather shabby warehouse type building: some from the street in front, some from behind, and some from side streets.

This was a "no-knock" warrant and search; so, the frontal assault took place simultaneously with the rear entry. Nothing about the entry was dainty. The heavy building doors caved in; the side windows were smashed; and a unit rappelled into the two-story building by crashing through a skylight. Every unit tossed flash-bang grenades in front of itself and was protected from the stinging smoke and blinding light by appropriate headgear.

The main room housed cubicles for 200 computers and their operators. None of them had the slightest inkling that a raid was about to surround them.

Col. Watson shouted through a bull horn, "Federal and State agents with a warrant. Step away from your computers and face the wall nearest you. Do not move. Do not attempt to alter your computer. Do not attempt to flee. Obey the orders of the officers."

He repeated the loud orders three times. The computer specialists complied with benumbed speed and alacrity. It was oddly quiet in the room except for the shuffling of hurried feet.

Sybil ran into the room and surveyed the computer stations to be certain that no one was hiding and attempting to use a computer to spread warnings to locations away from the Morgantown building. The paramilitary law enforcement personnel tensely guarded the employees while a group of very efficient and burly crime scene workers entered from all entrances and quickly began to empty the building of all electronics. The large room was bare of anything but teeth-chattering employees and tacky government metal furniture in ten minutes.

Sybil took the bull horn, "Who is in charge here?" she demanded.

For several minutes no one responded.

"Don't make me repeat myself. I am not a patient person. Obstinate silence will bring down on you a federal obstruction charge. *Capiche*??"

A meek geek among the FROGS [Front Office Girls] raised her hand timidly.

"Speak."

"I guess Mr. Chambers is the manager, but he's not here."

"Who is in charge now?" Sybil demanded brusquely.

"That'd be me, I guess," said a man with his nose plastered against the northwest wall.

"Come and face me...now!"

The man was middle-aged and looked like Joe Public in every respect—common in all respects.

"Name?"

"Jerry Jenkins, Ma'am."

"What do you do here, Jerry?"

"I'm kind of like the foreman. I handle staff issues like shift assignments, check on production, and trouble shoot."

"Big responsibility. Quickly tell me about the work that goes on here. We want to know about Beelzebub more than anything else. No one here should think they can withhold anything from me. Tell me the whole truth now or regret it very deeply later."

Sybil's delivery was the quintessential reason she was known by those who worked with her as "the snow queen" or sometimes "the ice queen". Nobody beneath her–except Lincoln–called her Sybil.

"I'm gonna take the Fifth unless you promise me immunity. I know a lot, and I know my rights. Before I say another word, I want a lawyer," Jerry said with color in his cheeks and defiance in his voice.

"This is federal and relates to a national emergency, Jerry. So, there's no 'fifth', but there is obstruction and lengthy interrogation if I don't get what I need here and now."

Jerry felt a good deal less defiant.

"I gotta have immunity. He'll kill me and my family. There's nothin' you can do that is worse that the Beelzebub character has done, believe you me."

"Make it good and quick, and I'll be fair about immunity, and I will throw in full protection for you and your family. Waste my time, and you will get a good long stay in the clink while multiple agencies prepare their cases against you. Your family will go it their own in that case."

Jerry did not doubt the seriousness of his tormentor. He was a rat caught in a corner by a herd of cats. There was no way out.

"Awright, awright, I'll spill it all. First of all, everybody in this room knows most of what I am tellin' you anyways. Nobody's an innocent. When you bleed me dry, you might wanna have chats with the other ring leaders."

He named them in front of everyone in the room in a voice that left nothing to question about what he had said and who he had ratted out. There was a significant amount of sweating, shivering, trembling, and foot shuffling, going on in the large room by the time he finished reciting his list. He was very complete and detailed and apparently not as dumb as he looked.

The law enforcement officers had their hands full that day. Two hundred persons of interest were interrogated by sixty officers accompanied by seventy-two court reporters and secretaries over eight hours. When they were finished, a lid of secrecy was clamped on the information; the two hundred employees were now suspects; and prison vans carted them all away to Fort Meade, Maryland where they had no means of communicating with the outside world—"for the duration" to use the Director of the Central Intelligence Agency's succinct decision.

What was learned was priceless and brought forth an imperative. The Morgantown facility manipulated the language, the communication, and the perceptions of people all over the world. This would have been quite benign if it was about selling soap or to convince an unsuspecting public that they needed a particular ambulance chaser to save them from the clutches of greedy insurance companies. It was not benign: rather, the exacting science of linguistics and its powerful partner, applied linguistics was being effectively utilized to convey misinformation—read here, "lies"—on a wholesale level with the most wicked of intents. The Morgantown facility employees–in concert with the Siemens co-conspirators–were able to create videos of President Vladimir Putin addressing his military generals; President Xi Jinping lecturing his powerful NPC [National People's Congress], and President Donald Trump telephoning from the Oval Office to 10 Downing to plot with Prime Minister Boris Johnson to undermine the economy of the UK.

In each of those dramas, terrible plots were being hatched to make the participants a cabal of dictators who would rule the world for their own gratification or a bunch of clowns creating the evidence for their own self-destruction, depending on the whims of the great unnamed puppeteer in the background's caprice. Every part of every communication collected as evidence was one hundred percent false, and the falsity was not just "fake news". It was so deftly and expertly created that the intonations, hints of dialects, facial and bodily movements, were identical to the real actions of the people portrayed. Computer renditions of thousands of videos of the "actors" speaking and performing were collated, sifted, and organized, so that any speech could come from any mouth with precise lip movements, facial expressions, enthusiasms, and angers. Heads could be transplanted; people could be aged or made younger; and messages inimitable to the well-being of the citizens of the world could be put into the mouths or pens of the world leaders of governments, churches, and political parties almost wholly undetectably.

It became abundantly clear that this grand scheme of deception and charade had been created by geniuses for the purposes of a very small handful of people—to make them rich, powerful, and feared beyond the success of any Hitler, Stalin, Genghis Khan, or Borgia Pope. Every law enforcement officer was dumbstruck by what applied linguistics had in its arsenal and the degree of manipulation of language and communication that was possible by the scholars of the science.

The officers learned that applied linguistics was going to be a force to deal with by law enforcement and the courts for a long time to come. The key difference between old fashion scholarly linguistics and applied linguistics is that while linguistics is the scientific study of the structure and development of language in general or of particular languages, applied linguistics focuses on the practical applications of language studies. It studies how language and communication can be manipulated for affect. Applied linguistics studies language as it affects real-life situations and how it can alter communication for better or worse. Sybil and her partners in this investigation all sincerely hoped this misapplication of a science was the worst they would ever see.

Beelzebub and his brilliant minions—whoever they all might be—had made ample misuse of the areas of applied linguistics that suited their malign purposes: phonetics—the study of speech and sounds; phonology—the study of the patterning of sounds; morphology–study of the structure of words. Moreover, the field of study identifies, investigates, and offers solutions to language-related problems and how to influence what is said. Applied linguistics is an interdisciplinary science which studies and influences a vast number of areas, some of which are directly related to linguistics, and others apply to language planning, policy, translation, conversation analysis, interlinguistics, stylistics, pragmatics, education, communication, sociology, and even anthropology—all of which were right up Beelzebub's nefarious alley.

That is, an applied linguist is not a grammarian or an historian and does not attempt to enforce rules within or impose rules on a language. Instead it is a science which concerns itself with observing and documenting language as it *is spoken* or *otherwise employed*, as in media, electronic transmissions, even sign language. It has incorporated principles that translate to practical machine translation software–or manipulation of recorded speech and other sounds–conversational (machine) agents–computer programs that can talk to a person like a "virtual nurse", a default dialer to shunt questioners to an information gathering tool; or in medicine, to ask or answer a number of health questions much the same way a physician's assistant would, and automatic question answering. It has led to text categorization—"spam v. not spam", acceptable standardization of "decent v. indecent speech or writing". The science of applied linguistics is capable of converting a collection of written or spoken material into machine-readable form which can be perverted into very realistic fake utterances by impersonated voices. Computational linguistics can be to linguistics what artificial intelligence is to computer science.

As in the case of Beelzebub and his minions, the science has advanced to an understanding and use of automated translation and human-machine interaction. Societies have grown up to further the principle mission of applied linguistics, i.e., to be a problem-driven field working towards the solution of language-related problems throughout the real world. Sybil gave a sigh which summed up the feelings about how these mercenary power-hungry monsters had perverted a truly useful science, much like Hitler's perversion of evolutionary science and genetics with the pseudoscience of eugenics which led to the holocaust.

By the time of the nightly news, six major news channels carried a new Beelzebub diatribe, obviously related to the raid in Morgantown, despite the stringent efforts by all agencies to keep a lid on it.

> *New York Times*, August 26
> Attention earthbound ignoramuses:
> I, Beelzebub, the Magnificent, declare that the efforts of the misguided fools of governments all over the world to interfere with my divine work will not be successful be they from the right or the left, the so-called educated or the simple true believers, by conservatives or liberals, by law enforcers or anarchists. I have enlisted the powers of Hades and his wife Persephone, Thanatos, and the Grand Master, Lucifer, himself. Be afraid. My time is near at hand.
> Signed: **Beelzebub, The Magnificent**
> Ha, ha, ha

An hour after the article dropped onto New York streets, bombings killed a total of 335 individuals in areas as disparate as Salt Lake City, Utah [Gay Pride Parade]; Mumbai, India [City wide protest against rape]; Batu Gajah, Malaysia [at the Kinta Golf Club during a reunion for all the alumni of the original Government English School—GES], Youngstown, Ohio [Zombi Apocalypse Annual Parade]; and Jeddah, Saudi Arabia [Meeting of the OPEC directors].

CHAPTER FOURTEEN

Beelzebub was not anxious about the raid in Morganstown, but he did see it as a move by his many enemies and a catalyst to push his agenda forward more rapidly. He knew he was getting very close to realizing his destiny. The amount of money streaming in from all of the cities, counties, regions, companies, and nations, who "did not negotiate with terrorists or extortionists" was making his organization more financially sound than ninety percent of the cities and countries of the world, more militarily powerful than all but the top twenty-two military countries, and possessing more devout followers from all stripes of life and ethnicity than any region he knew anything about. His greatest enthusiasm–at the moment–centered on finding just the right time and place to make his historical announcement.

It was becoming ever more clear that he had to dispose of the obnoxiously persistent directors of the FBI and the CIA. He could deal with the countercybertage agencies in his own time because he had a gathering of geniuses that would overpower all the others in an afternoon. It was a grand and elevating feeling to be so deeply aware of his own genius, his indisputable cleverness, his ability to recruit "to-the-death" followers and fighters of all colors, all races, all creeds, and all nationalities. He had always been the smartest guy in the room, the most charismatic, the most handsome and popular, and now the richest and most powerful. He had fooled everyone, and wouldn't they be kerfuffled when he made his announcement? Who could have guessed?

The six FBI agents assigned to surveil VPOTUS around the clock were getting bored and began to deplore the waste of resources and manpower for an obviously ill-thought out assignment. The man's life was a veritable open book. His monotonous schedule could have been programed for a robot: although he was not actually required to do so, Vice-President Broome attended the senate in his largely honorific constitutional position as the president of the senate, attended the National Security Council meetings almost every day, attended the weekly meetings of the Board of Directors of the Smithsonian Institution, and attended cabinet meetings more regularly than the president. His less formal, and more despised duties included going to weddings and funerals, talking to old ladies groups, meeting unofficially with industry and labor groups to show that President Willets held neither with favoritism, and taking junkets to undesirable foreign countries that the president declared himself to be "to busy to attend".

His social life was as minimal as he could make it. He preferred to talk to senators in his White House Office or in the seldom used, largely ceremonial, "Senate President's Office" in the Senate building. Otherwise, he kept to a mind-numbing schedule of traveling back and forth from the three-story Queen Anne style mansion built in 1893 on the grounds of the U.S. Naval Observatory to the front doors of the senate. Each day, after making his appearance in the senate chamber, he made a visit to the sculpture laboratory in the Senate basement to follow the progress of his portrait bust that would one day stand in the Senate wing of the United States Capitol. It greatly pleased him that his place in history was going to be immortalized under the terms of an 1886 Senate resolution which granted the honor to vice-presidents after finishing their terms.

V-P Broome had a good sense of humor and was often overheard telling self-deprecating jokes about the impotence of being vice-president. He like to quote his would-be and actual predecessors on the subject: When the Whig Party asked Daniel Webster to run for the vice presidency on Zachary Taylor's ticket in 1849, he replied "I do not propose to be buried until I am really dead and in my coffin." John Nance (Cactus Jack) Garner from Uvalde, Texas, who served as vice president from 1933 to 1941 under President Franklin D. Roosevelt, claimed that the vice presidency "isn't worth a pitcher of warm piss."

Harry Truman, who also served as vice president under Roosevelt, said that the office was as "useful as a cow's fifth teat." One advocate of having an amendment to the constitution to abolish the office of vice president, James Mitchell Ashley, stated on the floor of the senate that the office of vice president was "superfluous and dangerous." Randall Broome, the sitting VPOTUS, could not have agreed more with his predecessors, but he never showed the depths of his disdain.

The group of leaders of the manhunt for Beelzebub sat about in the conference room on the seventh floor of the George Herbert Walker Bush CIA building in Langley and groused about their failure to flush out their quarry or to prove his or her culpability.

DFBI Landon Murphy asked every member sitting in the handsome office, "Any ideas? I feel like I am sitting here with my thumb up my nose."

The room was silent until Sybil Norcroft suddenly flashed her famous and charismatic smile, "I have an idea. Maybe it is crazy, but it can't hurt; and who knows, it might just work."

She swore all the others to absolute secrecy. They shrugged or smiled depending upon their idea of whether or not her idea had any merit or chance of succeeding.

They all separated. When she got back to her office, Sybil put in a call to the personal office of the editor of the *Washington Post*.

The following morning, as usual, the three FBI agents assigned to watch the vice-president took seats in the gallery in different places than they did the day before. They wore different suits or dressed casually to prevent VPOTUS from taking notice of them. Then, they went to sleep with their eyes open as they had done for the past three and a half months.

The vice-president took his seat, shuffled his papers, put down his brief-case, and picked up his daily copy of the *Post* for a perfunctory look.

The headline slashed across the top of the front page would have brought an outcry from a lesser man, or stunned silence, or some other manifestation of the magnitude to the statement and its importance and implications.

He restrained his heightened emotions and glued his eyes to the page to avoid drawing attention to himself for the time being.

"VICE-PRESIDENT REVEALS HIMSELF TO BE THE MYTHICAL BEELZEBUB, ACKNOWLEDGES HIS SUCCESSFUL TAKEOVER OF THE PRESIDENCY, AND DELIVERS AN IMPROMPT ACCEPTANCE TO THE SENATE"

The headline was the same as it was the first three times he read it. He started to read the first view paragraphs of the article, which included a large flattering photograph of himself in front of a standing flag. The gist of the article was that the great American patriot and savior of the nation had almost single-handedly stepped in to quell the chaos going on in the country and the world, to gain the cooperation of the leaders of the United Nations and of our allies and former opponents. The third paragraph quoted the proposal which was put forth as a joint statement by the Speaker of the House, the Majority Leader of the Senate, and the Chairman of the Joint Chiefs of Staff.

"After lengthy negotiations in which the plight of the United States of America was deemed to be a failed nation, President Willets proffered his resignation and Vice-President Randall Broome was persuaded to take over in his stead. The legislators unanimously agreed to make a public offer–with all senior members of the press corps in attendance–to grant an unprecedented request for Mr. Broome to be named "President for Life" and to be addressed hereafter as "Your Majesty".

The new first officer of the United States looked out at the assembled senators, the full gallery, and the crowded press corps and calmed himself to appear humble, yet powerful.

His crumpling of the newspaper had drawn attention to him in the otherwise very quiet and sedate senate chamber. The majority leader got up from his front row seat and approached the VPOTUS.

"Is there anything you would care to say to the assembled senators, Mr. Broome? Every single member is in attendance today—a rare circumstance as befitting the occasion."

There was something about the leader's manner that was off-putting to the VPOTUS. He looked at the well-known senator with appropriate disdain, got up and walked to the microphone on the dais.

His eyes were misting. His fingers trembled slightly. However, he had rehearsed this speech as he had never done for any public utterance before in his long political career.

"Ladies and gentlemen of the world," he began. "I am sure you have been following the recent career of an individual heretofore known to you only as Beelzebub."

He made a little nervous cough, and an uncontrolled brief chuckle, "Ha, ha, ha."

Sybil crossed her fingers.

"My subjects. This is a red-letter day. No longer must I hide behind the cloak of my alter-ego, Beelzebub, the Magnificent. It appears that you here, governments around the world and the recognized leaders of industry, have finally come to your senses and realize what must be done, why it must be done, and who must do it.

"I humbly accept the title of President of the United States for Life asked of me. Of necessity, we will have a new capital city built in upstate New York to accommodate the business interests of the nation and the world. I will make further announcements by proclamation as necessary. Be prepared for great changes. I accept the challenges and know that you realize the revolutionary actions my comrades and I have had to make to get us to this point. We will write a new history in due time to acknowledge my leadership and their fine service under my instruction."

He looked at the roomful of bemused faces. There was something wrong with their expressions. Randall had expected jubilation or abject capitulation, but he was unprepared for expressions of disbelief, pity—was that really pity?—shock, and now faces with growing realization of what they were learning.

Sybil shook Granger Nelson's hand—the editor of the *Washington Post*—with whom she had faked the newspaper. He broke out laughing uproariously. She could not help herself; it was infectious; so, she laughed until she cried, a cathartic release. The chamber began to rock with laughter. Then, it all subsided as the magnitude of the crime they had heard the man confess struck them almost as a monolithic unit. The laughter became a choir of booing, hissing, and cursing.

The three FBI agents, and a squad of capitol police moved double-time towards the dais. A look of absolute consternation descended over Broome's face. His mind cleared enough to realize that the jig was up and that his grand plan now lay in ashes. He punched the majority leader in the face, leaped off the dais and disappeared through the unseen door in the rear of the chamber before the police officers could get to him. Sybil saw him escape, and her adrenaline took over. She jumped over chairs, pushed famous leaders aside as if she were a broken-field runner. The chaos and crowding in the area around the dais hampered her progress. She called to Lincoln for help, but he was enmeshed in the now stampeding crowd.

A young university student serving her senate clerkship recognized the DCIA and yelled to her, "Director Norcroft, this way."

Sybil could not hear the call.

"SYBIL!!!" the clerk screamed. Follow me. I know where he went!"

That call was as good as or better than anything else she had as an option; so, she ran towards the shrill voice.

"Sybil…this way!"

Sybil ignored the implicit disrespect of being addressed by her given name and pushed and shoved her way towards the beckoning girl.

"Lincoln, come with me. I think we have a way to get him."

The capitol was cordoned off by an army of police and marines who had been flown in from Fort Meade. The inside of the building was filling up with every kind of cop imaginable from chiefs of police down to pedestrian crosswalk guards. Broome could not possibly elude this feverish dragnet…but, he was gone.

"I'm Jen, Jennifer Mortensen, Madam Director. Trust me. Forget everyone else. We don't have time for me to explain, but I know the entrance to the secret tunnel. Run."

Sybil recognized a capable and self-assured leader when she saw one, even though Jen was no more than an eighteen-year-old farm girl from Nebraska or Podunk somewhere else. She stopped being the director and became the fleet follower.

Jen fiddled with an ornate knob in the capitol rotunda and flung open a door that Sybil had never had the faintest idea existed. The passageway was fairly narrow, but well-lit; and the floor was a smooth parquet which made running easy.

"Stop," Jen commanded. "Hear that?"

It took several seconds for Sybil to hear anything over the shrieking of her tortured lungs; but, yes, it was there. The unmistakable sound of running feet wearing hardsoled dress shoes. Before Jen could issue her next command, Lincoln caught up with them.

"What's up?" he gasped.

"Follow Jen, the next DCIA," Sybil said, smiling now that she had breath enough to speak.

Jen took off like an Olympic sprinter. Sybil looked at Lincoln with a small resigned shrug, and the two of them set out after the healthy young girl.

"What happens if Jen catches the monster?" Lincoln gasped out as they ran behind the fleet girl.

"I pity Beelzebub," Sybil said with a brief laugh owing to her shortness of breath.

Twenty-five yards ahead of them, the three pursuers heard the distinct opening and slamming shut of a heavy metal door. They asked of themselves more than it seemed that their bodies could provide, but they flew down the last few yards of the tunnel. Jen got there first—no surprise—and held the heavy door open for the two CIA agents, who flew past her.

"There he is," Jen shouted to her fellow pursuers, neither of whom was deaf, but they forgave her.

Lincoln and Jen were now in a sprint with Sybil calling for back-up on her Company iPhone. As predicted, Jen got to Broome first and executed a perfect flying tackle, totally heedless of her own safety. The VPOTUS—more recently spawn of the devil—was completely out of breath, and his heart was experiencing a thunderous tachycardia.

Jen sat on the fiend's back, and Lincoln slapped a set of zip-tie cuffs on Beelzebub's wrists.

"It's over," Lincoln said.

He gave Jen an exuberant hug much to the chagrin of both him and her, considering the possible Me-too implications.

"Sorry," he said, "but I didn't have words enough to tell you what a great woman you are. Maybe you really will be the next DCIA, like Dr. Norcroft said. Anyway, the whole human race owes you a good attaboy!"

Jen arched one eyebrow, and Lincoln, Sybil, and young Jennifer Mortensen, collapsed in inappropriate hysterical and thoroughly refreshing laughter.

Late the following morning—after the initial brouhaha died down—Sybil was sitting at home taking a well-earned rest on the couch with her no-longer worried husband, Charles, and daughter, Cerisse.

The red phone rang, and all three emitted a groan.

"Yes," Sybil said, then, "it is," and finally, "Thank you, Mr. President, I'll be there."

"So, Sybil, give," Charles said.

"Yes, Mom, no holding back," Cerisse pleaded.

Sybil treated her two favorite people in the world to an enigmatic Mona Lisa smile.

-THE END-

www.ingramcontent.com/pod-product-compliance
Lightning Source LLC
Chambersburg PA
CBHW072009170626
46813CB00005B/2082